I0668519

# The Wrong Husband

**Copyright: October, 2015**
Cover Design: The Killion Group, Inc.
Nancy Brophy
ISBN: 978-0-9862354-5-0

Contact Nancy at:
www.NancyBrophy.com
NancyBrophy@gmail.com

Other books Published by Nancy Brophy:

Plotting Your Story Arc, Workbook for Fiction Writers, Plotters and Pantsers

Fiction:
Hell On The Heart
The Wrong Brother
The Wrong Hero
The Wrong Cop
The Wrong Lover

# The Wrong Series

Each SEAL team member has a core belief that has led him to become the best of the best. No one becomes a SEAL for public adoration. Acknowledgment doesn't happen, at least not on an individual level. Becoming a SEAL team member is almost impossible. Only a very few achieve it.

Once in, the decision to leave is gut wrenching. If one chooses to not make the Navy a lifetime commitment, then who is he? Who will he become? Will he ever achieve the same satisfaction, beyond being an adrenaline junkie, in another career?

This series is about men who are former SEALs. These are stories of men who struggle to transfer their beliefs, values and training into careers as private civilians while retaining the same sense of dedication and honor.

Book 4, The Wrong Husband is the story of Austin Stevens and his struggle to leave his past behind and become the man he was destined to be.

Book 1 –
# The Wrong Brother
Zack and Chloe

*This is what lying got you – the wrong brother.*

Book 2 –
# The Wrong Hero
Travis and Abby

*"If this is a chess game, the one thing you should have been able to predict is that the queen always protects the king.*

Book 3 –
# The Wrong Cop
Grant and Dori

*"It pisses me off I'm attracted to you." His erection betrayed his words.*

*He was lying, but so was she. "You're like the wad of gum on the sole of my shoe. Only worth as much consideration as it takes to get rid of you."*

Book 3.5 - Bonus book –
## The Wrong Lover
Marshall and Lily

*Her brown eyes and raspy voice stayed with him. Her taste lingered on his lips. After this fiasco was over, he'd find her. All he knew was that her name was Lily, but it wasn't her name he was after.*

Book 4 –
## THE WRONG HUSBAND
Austin and Nicole

*"It's a vacation and we are going to have a fabulous time."*

Book 5 –
## THE WRONG SEAL
Sam and Imogene

*She had no idea how lucky she'd been to be raised in a place where crazy people weren't running the circus.*

# The Wrong Husband

Nancy Brophy

# Chapter One

*Wednesday, January 4th*
*San Diego, California*

Elena Vasquez should have arrived by now.

Nicole Layton scraped the sand from the soles of her shoes onto the hard rubber mat. Her walk on the beach had firmed her wavering determination. Not only was her decision the right one – it was her only choice.

The beige brick building that imprisoned her niece offended her. With luck, she'd never have to visit another medical institution again. Gritting her teeth, she glanced at her watch, then hip-checked the blue metal blue wheelchair emblem and watched the door creep open in an agonizingly slow movement. Normally, her impatience would override the mechanics, but currently she had nothing to do but wait. And hope. And pray.

Gunter Gustafson, her husband's burly bodyguard and heartless minion had accompanied her to southern California. Traveling alone was forbidden, along with a host of other activities. Some of the never-ending rules were important, but most were arbitrary. Senator Linus Layton liked control over all his possessions, his wife among them.

Nicole understood the need for security. Her husband was a wealthy, powerful man, which made her a valuable target. But his safety precautions chafed to the point she felt less protected and more like his prisoner. There was no doubt if she displeased him, he would have her locked away as he had her beautiful five-year-old niece, Libby. Thinking about her husband, fifteen hundred miles away still made her heart race and pulse jump.

She could well imagine his anger escalating out of control. Bruises and broken bones would no longer be enough. Nothing would satisfy him until he killed her and somehow even her death would be her fault.

Getting away from Linus was her number two priority. Protecting Libby was number one.

Gunter was a big man, not tall, but solid. Nicole had laced his coffee with sleeping pills, worrying the entire time about dosage. Were four enough? Were six too many? She settled on grinding five pills to a fine dust before adding them to her thermos.

Uncertain how much time was required for the drugs to kick in, she'd poured the coffee for him as he'd exited the expressway. Three blocks later, he'd barely put the car in park before he'd yawned and collapsed into a deep slumber.

Her next question was how long would be he incapacitated? His snore rumbled like a volcanic eruption and encouraged her to think she had adequate time. Crossing her fingers, she sent a small prayer heavenward that nothing would go wrong.

Her plan had to work.

A battered Honda pulled into the circular driveway of the private medical facility. Elena had arrived. Late, but she'd come, and that was the important thing. If Nicole hadn't known of her former nanny's desperate financial situation, she doubted words would have persuaded her.

The sun-blasted maroon beater squeezed into a spot reserved for ambulances causing Nicole to choke back a laugh. Elena still lived life on her own terms.

The short, round South American woman marched with a determined step. Nicole held the door open.

"You're hurt," Elena announced three feet shy of the threshold, worry reflected in her deep brown eyes. Nicole had known this meeting would be difficult, but her stamina flagged.

She put a finger to her lips to remind the older woman to lower her voice. "I'm fine. These are old injuries." Leaning in, she kissed her childhood nanny in welcome, wincing from the other woman's firm hug. "It's been too long since we've seen each other. I wish we had more time today."

Except for the gray streaks in her long dark braid bound at her nape, the woman looked the same as she had twenty-one years earlier. She'd been the caretaker to both Nicole and her younger sister, Beth.

"I don't like this situation," Elena grumbled but lowered her voice to a whisper. "It reminds me of –"

"The past is best forgotten." Nicole refused to discuss that summer, or the humiliation that followed. She thrust the briefcase toward the shorter woman. "Here is enough money to take care of you and Libby for at least two years. If the child proves too difficult, there is enough to provide her with professional care."

Elena sniffed, offended. "You think a five-year-old girl is too much for me?"

Tears pricked her eyes and Nicole bit her bottom lip as she squeezed her hands together. "Libby hasn't been right since the accident. The doctors tell me she is getting worse. You may have to make choices you don't want to make."

She didn't add that her husband's physicians didn't expect the child to live another two years. A fact Nicole refused to believe since they routinely predicted Libby's doom. Elena didn't need to know her aggravations because if their diagnoses proved to be true, nothing could be done.

Elena pulled her into her arms as if she were still a child and held her close. "Like the choices you are making now," she murmured. "Everything will be okay. This man, this Senator, he gave you the money?"

Nicole shook her head. "I took it. Libby must be safe. We are leaving on a vacation in a few days. He won't discover the money is missing until he returns." Behind her back she clenched her fists, crossed her fingers and hoped her prophesy would be true.

The nanny's sharp eyes missed very little. "Is he mean to you?"

Nicole hated to admit the truth aloud, but it was essential that Elena understand if things went wrong... She took a deep breath and acknowledged the facts inwardly. If things went wrong, she would be dead. "I'm leaving him. I had to protect Beth's daughter first." Even now, she couldn't bring herself to admit the consequences if the game she played fell apart. "Let's go get Libby."

Elena's face brightened. Nicole released a silent prayer of gratitude. She was doing the right thing. Her husband wouldn't be able to use

Libby as a pawn.

"You will come to Argentina when you can?"

"As soon as it is safe." Nicole hoped her words wouldn't turn out to be a lie.

# Chapter Two

*Lake Forest, Illinois*
*Friday, January 6th*

*It was the season of light and the season of darkness.*

Austin Stephens wasn't usually a man who quoted Dickens, but following his new client into his library put him in that frame of mind. Growing up with a father who had derided him for having his nose in a book did not inspire literary quotes.

Illinois Senator Linus Layton gestured toward the leather couches, choosing the shorter of the two for himself. Neither Austin, nor his brother Travis preferred to sit with their back to an open door, but the half-smile on the older man's face made Austin believe this was a test of sorts.

He wanted to laugh. The brothers had lived in a dangerous environment damn-near every day of their life, sitting with a back to a wall wouldn't save anybody when real problems erupted.

The book-lined walls implied a man of learning and thoughtful pursuits, but the man reeked of paranoia and obsession, wanting each of his twenty-two rooms wired with both cameras and microphones. A strange anxiety, since only he and his trophy wife, lived in this sprawling mock English Tudor monstrosity. Austin understood the difference between security and spying and he suspected Layton did as well.

What was it about the Senator that made his skin crawl? The man's short, barrel-chested, well-dressed frame screamed well-to-do. Somewhere in his mid-fifties, he still sported a full head of dark hair highlighted with a few silver streaks at the temples. In photos, he looked happy and healthy, thanks in part to his artificial tan and much younger, blonde, stunningly beautiful, and adoring wife.

The bruised knuckles on the older man's right hand surprised him. Bruised knuckles indicated contact, but the man's persona did not invite intrusion into his personal space.

The things he wanted done to the house, Stephens Security could easily accomplish and were within the scope of their normal duties. The company jointly owned by Austin and his older brother, Travis still struggled to cement its place as a serious contender in the overcrowded field of private corporate protection.

Scuttlebutt on the street indicated the Senator was dipping his toe into the water of higher political office. Working for a Presidential candidate would open an entirely new revenue stream.

He and Travis had eagerly flown to Illinois early that morning, hoping to snag a new influential client. Now that they were here, every instinct warned the bait had a hidden hook.

The door from the kitchen tucked between deep bookcases opened silently. Had his attention been elsewhere he might have missed the change in air currents.

Unlike many people used to being in the spotlight, Nicole Layton entered the darkened alcove at the rear of the room and stopped. Even across the room, he read the indecision in her body movements as she reached for the door that had closed behind her. Aware she'd been spotted or maybe fearing a retreat would be worse, she dropped her arm and pressed forward, slipping around the perimeter keeping to the shadows. Her gaze was on the floor as she moved with quick steps.

"Nicole, darling, you're here. How delightful." Linus stretched a languid hand of welcome over the back of the couch but remained seated.

Austin's respect for the other man's awareness increased, but he also noted the public face of the marriage took a different turn in private. Nothing in her expression echoed her husband's words of delight. But by the time she'd stepped into the sunlight, she'd donned a mask of studied politeness.

The photos hadn't lied. She was a stunner. He'd been prepared for her beauty, but the impact of her presence hit him like a sucker punch. As though a siren had beckoned, he was half out of his seat before he realized he'd moved. The Senator's attention was on his wife and had missed his telling error in judgment.

His brother rose seconds behind him. A quick glance at the amusement etching brother's expression confirmed his suspicions. Travis was fully aware of his faux pas.

The only other person who saw his misstep was the wife, but her focus was on her husband's outstretched hand. With a brief hesitation and a quick dilation of her eyes, she crossed the room.

Her white-blonde hair was piled high on her head and allowed to descend in random ringlets. She was without a doubt the most beautiful woman he'd ever seen − a magnetic presence that pulled at his core so powerfully he feared it would suck his soul from his body.

His scalp tingled. He spread his stance and narrowed his eyes, needing to control his response. Never had anyone affected him in such a manner. Had he been alone he would have twisted his neck from side-to-side to relax his body.

Her face was delicate with large heavily lashed eyes, perfect skin, and shiny lips painted an enticing shade of rose. Thirty-three according to her bio but the conservative suit pegged her as older. Her slightly puffy blue eyes held an inner circle of distress and her smile reeked of insincerity. Her perfume was subtle, but her real scent was of money and tightly laced sexual attraction. Expensive, well-tailored clothes and the tall, sexy heels begged a man to admire her legs and the ass attached. And Austin was a man fully prepared to do that with any woman other than the one standing in front of him.

"I didn't mean to interrupt. I hadn't realized you were using this room." Her voice held a light, lilting quality that belied her actions.

Layton chuckled, a sound without mirth. "Not a problem. I'm always delighted to have you by my side."

She stilled. "If you're sure."

Her walk was slow, each step carefully measured. White lines appeared around her mouth, and her breath developed a slight, almost undetectable hitch.

She stretched an arm across the narrow coffee table to shake hands. The sleeve of her designer suit rose. Recent blue and purple bruises appeared on her wrist. Her polished nails, the exact color of her suit, were unbroken. She'd been tied or held, preventing her from retaliating. Whatever had happened to her hadn't been a spur of the moment splash of anger, but deliberate, thought-out and cruel.

As their hands touched, jolts of awareness zipped up his arm. Her focus, which had been primarily on his chin lifted to his eyes, then fell to the floor as she murmured a greeting.

Austin cast a sideward glance. Only someone who knew his brother well would recognize that behind his noncommittal face was anger. Both hated men who used women and children for punching bags. Ignore the fact her husband wanted to hire Stephens Security. It was his wife who was in desperate need of their help.

The Senator patted the couch, indicating she was to sit next to him. "How was the visit to your doctor?"

While she appeared to do what he'd requested, Austin noted she positioned herself on the edge. The rigid back pinned her as the poster child for excellent posture. Cleverly she angled her body to look directly at Linus, the sun of her Universe. But he'd seen enough abused women to know her real intent was to keep at least an arm's length away from hands that inflicted pain.

"Fine." Her Mona Lisa smile never faltered.

The Senator's heavy brows drew together as he studied her face. "Nothing broken?"

Austin gritted his teeth as the Senator's words appeared solicitous, but expression screamed disappointment. Behind the mask of civility he'd witnessed a brief glimpse of the dark side of a public personality.

Awareness hit him solidly in the gut. The Senator was proud. In some misguided man-of-the-people façade, Senator Linus F. Layton plainly showed he was the husband he expected his security team to be. A man's man, as assholes like to say.

His father had bragged to his two young sons about training his wife to be obedient through brute force. He, too, was a man's man. Austin rejoiced that he was dead.

Nicole dusted some non-existent lint off her skirt with the back of her hand. "Minor bruising."

She chose to play it cool, but she might as well have emasculated the little tyrant judging by his frown. "My wife tumbled down a flight of stairs last night. We were quite worried." He reached for her hand, but she ratcheted her body to face the men across the table and avoid his touch.

"I've been so clumsy. I must pay more attention to where I step."

The move cost her. Austin read the pain in her eyes. He'd bet his next paycheck that there had been more than bruising to her ribcage. The Senator was twice widowed. She was his third wife. Boy, had she chosen badly.

"You've been so brave. I got you a little gift." From the side table, Layton lifted a blue rectangular Tiffany box and thrust it toward his wife.

She masked her hesitation by clasping her hands to her cheeks in rehearsed surprise. "You shouldn't have."

He continued to extend his arm holding the gift. "Open it." His words were a command.

Nicole lifted the lid and a black-hinged case slid out. A practiced look of delight lit her face seconds before she had time to register the contents.

"Pearls," she said. "Three strands. They're beautiful."

Austin didn't know much about jewelry, but he had a strong handle on women. A cool blonde needed a spark, a dash of color. Nobody in this day and age, unless they were over the age of sixty wore Barbara Bush pearls. At least not among the women he dated.

No wonder she looked older than thirty-three.

Why didn't she leave? Austin snorted inwardly. The reasons were as complex as the women involved. While the public thought physical abuse only happened in a lower socio-economic group, the woman sitting across from them shattered that myth.

"You have a lovely home," he said when the silence lingered.

"Thank you." She played her role as the political wife to perfection. She favored the Senator with a smile. "My husband has superb taste."

Layton chuckled. His chest puffed as he preened like a peacock. "Of course, I picked you."

Another minute of this farce and Austin would bolt for the door. Everything about her cried out to him. "Mrs. Layton, I've been sitting here, looking through the doorway at your extensive porcelain compilation."

The Senator raised an eyebrow.

*That's right, I'm using the big words, you effete snob.*

He continued addressing the repugnant man's wife. "I must confess I have an avid interest in china patterns. Would you mind showing me your collection?"

She played it perfectly, waiting for a slight incline of Layton's head, before she rose. "Please call me Nicole. I'd be delighted to guide you through the room."

Austin offered his arm, not from an outdated notion of chivalry, but he suspected the support was necessary. Any movement had to be tortuous. How had her doctor allowed her to return home?

The Senator inched to the edge of the couch, prepared to follow, but Travis stopped him with a low murmured phrase. "While we're alone we can finish the details of your request."

Despite her long legs, Austin shortened his steps. Iraq had screwed with his hearing, yet he caught a small but sharp inhale with each step that sent empathy through every cell in his body. As remarkable as her courage was, he hoped she possessed the fortitude to live without the trappings of wealth her marriage provided. "My grandmother once told me that one way you could tell fine china was if it was thin enough to read through."

Nicole stumbled, allowing him to take more of her weight. He patted her arm in encouragement.

She recovered faster than he'd anticipated. "I don't believe I've ever heard that."

The room was lined with glass cabinets,

displaying and sheltering hundreds of patterns of place settings. In his wildest dreams, he couldn't imagine anyone wasting their time and resources on something as meaningless as dishware.

"The Laytons have collected place settings for centuries. The family has a more extensive collection of White House patterns than the White House itself."

*Who the hell cared? She had a lot more important things to worry about than china, but he was cautious. Not every woman in jeopardy wanted to be rescued. Was being a Senator's wife worth the price she paid? Maybe to her it was. Some women, even beautiful ones, didn't know their value.* "Do you have a favorite?"

"I prefer the clean lines of 20th-century Presidential choices more than the early ones. Woodrow Wilson's is my personal favorite."

They walked into the room, stopping frequently to admire one setting or another. In heels, they were almost eye-to-eye. He liked a tall woman, but he bet the Senator hated being the shorter of the two.

Another door from the kitchen banked one wall. The glass reflected a brawny man eavesdropping on their conversation.

Austin angled his body to shield her from his view. "The man in the kitchen. Your bodyguard?" He stood close enough to her ear to mouth the words without sound.

Her gaze glanced around the room, careful not to make any quick movements. Was she looking for spies? Or an escape? She stood taller and a coolness settled in her expression before bobbed her head in a whisper of a nod.

He pressed hard, knowing his time was short. "Do you trust him?" This time her head twitched with the barest of motions. Just as he suspected, she lived in an isolated world. "You're in danger. I can help."

Her eyes - no true shade of blue, but not green either, a stunning shade of teal would be the closest - stared into his. Her expression was so panicked he feared she'd scream. The hand resting in the crook of his arm tightened as her glance took in every corner of the room searching for hidden dangers. If he had more time, he could help her deal with her stress. Years as a SEAL had taught him some useful tricks, but for now he had to get her out of here.

He leaned closer, knowing he had to make her position clear. "Your husband is escalating, putting cameras and microphones in every room. You'll be his prisoner."

She shook her head so violently the loose tendrils bounced as she placed her hand on his chest. "Please. Don't speak." Her voice was barely above a whisper, but every cell of her being vibrated with intent.

Being silent was the last thing she needed. "How many times have you gone to a hospital for your clumsiness in past few months? Twice? Six times? You've got to get out of this situation."

Her gaze once again took in every corner of the room. "There's nothing you can do."

Austin pressed his lips together. He wanted to cradle her in his arms, toss her over his shoulder and snatch her from the house. "He's already buried two wives. I would hate to see you be a third. Take my card." He thrust it into her hand.

"Here you are." The Senator's voice came from behind, interrupting any further conversation. Nicole's entire body jerked at the sound.

Austin turned to see his brother trailing in the shorter man's wake. "We were discussing the Bush's taste in dishware as opposed to the Clintons."

The Senator beamed. "I suspect for a man of your military background that you might have a preference on more levels than one."

Austin didn't bother to mention he was apolitical and never voted. "Mrs. Layton is quite knowledgeable about your collection. It was truly a delight to view the room with her."

"Nicole, please," she insisted, her cheeks pink from the compliment.

Layton eyed her hand still tucked into the fold of Austin's arm. The Senator's gaze held a second or two longer than necessary before he returned his attention to Travis to ask, "Will you need to see the rest of the house?"

Nicole trembled and slipped her hand free as Travis assured the man that a set of floor plans would suffice. The Senator nodded pleasantly.

"You look pale, my dear. Perhaps a short rest would do you good."

"Yes. Thank you." While her tone was clipped and formal, she couldn't back to the door fast enough. "It was nice to meet you," she said without a shred of sincerity, but Austin noted his card had disappeared to a hiding place somewhere on her body.

"You, too, Mrs. Layton," the brothers said in unison.

The Senator's eyes narrowed and a sly smile curled the corner of his lips. Austin stuck his clenched fist into the pocket of his slacks. By offering help, he had put Nicole in more danger. He had to do something to swing the pendulum back, so she wouldn't be punished for his actions.

"Gunter," the Senator said, his voice raised

for show.

The guard who'd listened at the door stepped into the room. Austin knew exactly who and what he was by the short, compact body, scarred face and arms that swung wide and couldn't quite touch the sides of his body when he walked. A fighter, a street brawler, or possibly a semi-pro who'd lost in the ring, but hadn't yet gone to seed. His size and stance radiated his contempt for weakness.

Even though the Senator had turned, Austin smiled invitingly at the guard. In return, the beefy man scowled. Layton's head swiveled and his gaze scrutinized the interaction between them. Austin gave a lingering appreciative glance of interest before refocusing on the others.

Travis busied himself by studying the floor, but Austin knew he fought laughter. Layton's speculative look provided insight into his personality. The man's trade was secrets. He had something on his wife, and Austin vowed to find out what.

"I'll look for your bid tomorrow. Nicole and I are leaving on a Mediterranean cruise. I would like the work done while we're gone. Gunter will be your contact."

"Oh, good," Austin murmured audibly beneath his breath and smiled in the

bodyguard's direction a final time. Gunter
visibly recoiled.

# Chapter Three

*Friday, January 13th*
*Civitavecchia, Italy*

Friday the thirteenth. Why would anyone set sail on such a day? But when her husband had booked the trip – months earlier – in celebration of their third anniversary, Nicole had never uttered one word of disapproval. Nor had she expected to be accompanied all over Italy by not one guard but two.

Her paranoid husband had changed his mind and arranged for Gunter to be included at the last minute. Why? Did Linus know about San Diego? She'd been a trembling wreck since they'd left the States.

At the dock, the Costa Concordia, the largest ship in the Italian line sparkled in the dappled sunlight, dwarfing the workers on shore scurrying to prepare the vessel.

Bad omens, be damned. This was her only possibility of escape, and she'd spent hours readying herself. Her plan was to succeed or die trying.

A crisp snap in the air had the multi-national passengers crowding inside the sparsely furnished boarding terminal. She squeezed behind a large group of sturdy Germans. Once out of eyesight, she slipped off of the ridiculous heels she'd worn to please her husband and slumped against the wall for a temporary reprieve while the Senator argued with the Italian authorities. For the few moments she was hidden from his view, a smile or an adoring gaze wasn't required. She allowed herself the luxury of a brief catnap.

Linus had chosen an Italian line to avoid the paparazzi, but since they'd arrived in Rome three days earlier he'd done everything in his power to attract attention – including arranging a meeting with the Pope. Now he created a scene because they, like the hundreds of other passengers who had arrived early, were forced to wait until the ship was ready to board.

Consternation zipped through the crowd, a palpable emotion. An elbow brushed against her arm. She opened her eyes, stepped into her shoes, and dredged up a plastic smile. Joaquin and Gunter parted the waves of passengers in a frantic search. Obviously, her husband had noticed she was missing and his army had been dispatched to locate her.

She noted the relief that crossed Gunter's face when he spotted her in the crowd. She smiled pleasantly, hoping to make his worries appear foolish. As it was, his trust level was minimal. He hadn't believed he'd passed out in San Diego as she'd claimed, but neither had he reported the nap to her husband. She suggested a doctor's visit in case of a brain tumor and had the satisfaction of seeing his panicked expression.

Her goal was to quietly sever the leash without anyone being the wiser. She carried a vial of ground sleeping pills in case she needed to drug either or both guards. No one would stand in her way.

Linus's smile was triumphant when she rejoined him. "The Italian authorities are going to allow us to board first."

*Of course, they were. They want us out of their hair.*

"How nice," she said.

Standing in the shadow of the ship reminded her how insignificant she was in the world. Who would miss an unimportant woman? Quickly she tamped down the small delight that crept to her lips as they climbed the ramp to enter the vessel.

The carpeted lobby was elegant with a flowering ceiling of blown glass anemones. Linus nodded his approval as he led the way. Glass elevators whisked them to the Germania deck. Nicole relaxed. Even the annoying shoes that pinched her toes ceased to be a problem.

Linus's happiness would ease the way for her escape.

"Are the two rooms identical?" she asked as they approached the end of the long hallway.

"We'll see." He gestured to Gunter who trotted down the corridor ahead of them to open the doors. Joaquin lagged behind, carrying their personal luggage which the Senator had refused to let the ship handle. "I had no idea you needed eight suitcases of clothes. A tiny bit excessive, don't you think?"

His face was that of his public persona and told her nothing. She forced a smile.

"I wanted to be prepared for any occasion. Next time I'll know what to expect."

"Of course. You've never cruised before."

The interior of the cabins was a relief. Linus choose the right one. She desperately wished she could lock herself inside and bolt the doors.

The gray sky cast shadows through the open balcony doors. Nicole hurried to the deck and peered over the railing. The drop to the dark and murky sea below was significantly farther than she'd envisioned. But none of that mattered. Blood surged through her veins. A lightheaded feeling of elation came over her as she inhaled the salty sea air.

"Let's tour the ship," her husband called from the cabin's interior.

Ready-made excuses leaped to her lips. "Our clothes need to be hung up and aired out. You'll hate wearing a wrinkled tux." She was desperate for time alone to get everything in place. Stepping inside the room, she closed and locked the door behind her.

Linus rolled his eyes. "Gunter can unpack."

Nicole wrinkled her nose. "I can't stand the thought of his hands in my underwear." She had no idea whether Gunter's proclivities ran to the perverse, but her husband's snobbery would allow him to believe it.

Her comment stopped him short. "I had no idea you felt that way." A mean chuckle followed. She swallowed, careful to keep her face averted. Linus had the ability to unerringly poke at a weakness.

He moved about the cabin as he spoke, opening drawers and checking out the suite. "I suppose you would have preferred the gay guard I refused to hire."

*One of the guards was gay?*

She maintained a disinterested tone. "Who do you mean?"

"You met him – the one who was so taken by the china."

Nicole's gaze met her husband's superior sneer. She had not categorized Austin Stephens as gay. In fact, his masculinity had made her nervous in a way she hadn't been for quite a while. Had she misread him?

"You didn't know? That was the reason I put off having the house done. Imagine how my political base would feel about my hiring fags."

She hurried to change the subject before he launched into a lengthy spiel about homosexuality which would only serve to anger her. "There's a cigar bar on the fourth floor."

His eyes lit with anticipation, then faded. "You know I don't smoke anymore."

She tilted her head. "In America. Europeans have different attitudes. And cigars aren't really smoking." How many times had she heard her father-in-law say those words as he puffed away on a stogie at the dinner table?

He hesitated. She didn't push. Instead she opened a suitcase, pulled out a sports jacket and snapped it several times to ease the wrinkles.

A frown crossed Linus' face. He was annoyed that she'd had things to do which might interfere with his plans. "I'll leave Joaquin with you."

"Outside the door, please."

The Senator glanced about the room, scanning for hidden dangers.

"The patio's locked. A good Cuban and a glass of single malt scotch will relax you. This, after all is a vacation." She glanced at the gray sky and infused her voice with optimism. "And we are going to have a fabulous time."

He chuckled. "If I'd realized you felt that way we would have scheduled a trip sooner." He walked the five steps that separated them and leaned in for a perfunctory kiss. His dry lips barely brushed hers. Yet she steeled her body to keep from recoiling.

Briefly, she considered urging him to hurry back, but didn't. The words were out of character for her. His staff snickered behind their hands, calling her a frigid bitch. And she'd encouraged them by frowning if someone touched her even accidentally.

Linus, much to her relief, hadn't approached her since the previous week when he'd lost his temper and beaten her. She didn't want him to start now. Her ribs still ached with any sudden movement. She'd taken her pain pills sparingly, hoping to make them last until she really needed them.

Several days loomed ahead before they made it to Barcelona. Her fluent Spanish made Spain the logical escape route, easier to blend into the countryside and hide.

Dutifully she walked her husband to the door, not to see him off, but to make sure the lock was secured behind him.

As soon as he'd disappeared, she dug

through the stack of almost empty suitcases and pulled up the ones she needed. The ship sailed at five o'clock, but it was possible the bars weren't open and her husband would return sooner than planned.

◇

Linus was drunk. The sour scent of bourbon oozed through his pores and lingered in the air. Never a stumbling drunk, his posture remained perfect but the slight slur to his words worried her. When inebriated her husband turned vicious.

He'd spent the afternoon trolling the ship's bars and now struggled into a tux. The cabin would never have been described as spacious, but now the closeness of the room suffocated her. She applied her makeup with care. Anything wrong could cause him to fly into a rage.

His grunting increased as he struggled with the buttons on his starched shirt. She crossed the room as silently as possible and reached for one of her three long black dresses. "We could order room service, if you'd prefer."

The ship's itinerary advertised the first night as casual dining. She hurried, hating to stand in front of him in her underwear out of fear he'd decide now was the time to become amorous.

"Jesus, you're such a skinny bitch. Good

thing you've got a pretty face 'cause that body would put off any man."

With the dress covering her face she blinked back tears of hurt, marveling at his ability to get to her.

"You gonna wear that elastic bandage around your ribs the entire trip? You want people to feel sorry for you."

She struggled to find a calm voice that didn't betray her emotions. "The doctor said I was to wear it until the end of the month, but if it bothers you I won't wear it during the day."

"Oh, no," his tone dripped with sarcasm, "if the doctor told you to wear it, then by all means, do. I won't be responsible if you hurt yourself."

Nor would he be responsible if he was the one who hurt her.

He thrust his arm toward her and it took every instinct she possessed not to jump back when all he wanted was his cuff stud fastened. Fortunately for her, he didn't notice her revulsion.

"You look very nice," she said to sooth him. He accepted her words as his due with a curt nod.

"I thought we'd try the Peking duck tonight."

"Perfect."

Compared to the Tommy Bahama casual the

rest of the passengers wore, Nicole felt uncomfortably overdressed, but she'd been there before. Her husband's insistence upon formal attire was legendary. Even in Washington, he was out-of-place in that regard.

They found the dining room without any problems other than others stared and whispered behind their hands. She and Linus led the parade with Gunter and Joaquin trailing behind. Both guards was a snarl and while one couldn't see the gun in their hands it didn't take much to imagine it. America's reputation as a gun-loving nation was fully cemented.

They were barely seated – with Joaquin posted outside the front door and Gunter located near the kitchen – when Linus ordered his first drink, then a second. Her heart sank. Eating dinner in silence was not unusual at home, but in public they put a social face on it.

Her napkin wiped the sweat that beaded on her upper lip. Her ribs ached, forcing each breath to be slow and carefully drawn. The first time they fought, he'd blackened her eye and split her lip. Since then, he'd been careful not to damage her face. Her arms and ribs had taken the brunt of his anger.

He finished his drink and stared unseeing at his meal. Her stomach lurched. If he hit her again she might be too weak to leave. That guard. That security guard. The gay one. What had he said? *He's already buried two wives. I would hate to see you be a third.*

She gritted her teeth. As Linus tightened all her avenues of escape, it might be months before she had another opportunity and once he discovered the missing money from his safe, he would erupt in fury.

"Another cocktail, sir?" a uniformed server asked.

Her husband chuckled and flashed his Senatorial smile. "No. One more and I won't be able to dance with my wife."

The men laughed as if they shared a secret, while Nicole worked to hide her dismay. Dancing? Tonight? Her heels were too high. One more thing to anger him.

She gave a practiced smile. "The motion of the boat—"

"Ship," her husband's haughty tone conveyed his feelings.

"Ship," she corrected, "is making me queasy. If we're going to dance I want to run to the room and put on a motion patch."

He frowned and her stomach lurched. "Send Gunter."

She gave pause like she was considering his idea, then shook her head. "No, I don't remember where I put them. Besides, I'll be back before you're done. You've barely touched your meal."

The alcohol made his reaction slower than normal. He fumbled a bit, finally nodding his agreement. "Take… " he flicked his fingers in Joaquin's direction unable to recall the guard's name.

"Of course." She was out of her seat before he could change his mind.

From the corner of her vision she saw Gunter rise from his table by the kitchen to intercept her at the entrance to the restaurant. "Ma'am," his voice was a harsh bark.

Ma'am was such a funny word. She hated being ma'am-ed. People rarely meant it as a compliment. But tonight the word infused her backbone with steel. She turned and leveled a condescending look at the guard who had dared to alter her course of action.

"I'm running to the room for a motion-sickness patch. Stay with the Senator. Try to keep him from ordering more alcohol. Joaquin, come with me."

Neither guard liked her, but both were used to following orders. Gunter scowled, but the shorter of the two men, Joaquin fell in behind her.

She'd miscalculated, figuring she had a week to leave the ship. If she didn't leave now, he'd make it impossible. Halfway to the elevator a new plan occurred to her.

Linus didn't pay his guards to think. All they had to do to collect their substantial salaries was follow his orders, take his verbal abuse, and accept petty assignments like washing cars and picking up dry cleaning without comment or complaint.

The lobby was devoid of passengers as they stepped into the glass elevator. Nicole pushed the button. Barely had the doors closed when she clutched her stomach and collapsed to her knees.

Joaquin grasped her upper arm to tug her upright. "What? Are you sick?"

Nicole made a retching sound. In response the man, paid to guard her life, dropped her arm and leapt backward.

"I'm having cramps."

"Cramps?" Relief evident in his tone. "That's nothing. They'll pass."

"Not without medication and I didn't bring any. We have to find a shop that sells it." Purposely she moaned low and long before turning her head to see if he was buying her act.

He was. An anxious expression betrayed his thoughts as he frantically searched the elevator ceiling for a solution. "Right now?"

"Yes." Another moan. "I don't care if the

Senator is furious."

Panic was written plainly on his face. No one wanted to see her husband angry.

"All right. Let's go." He reached for her arm a second time but stopped when she knelt even lower and touched her forehead to the carpeted floor.

"I need to lie down for a few minutes."

His shoes shuffled back and forth. "I tell you what. I'll get you to the room then go find the medicine."

The elevator door opened on the tenth floor.

"No," she said straightening cautiously. "Everyone's at dinner. I can get to the room alone. You go find the medicine. Surely by the time you get back I'll be able to leave. Hurry."

She pushed a button for a lower floor, knowing it wasn't the correct one, staggered out of the elevator clutching her stomach, and wondered briefly how long it would take him to remember the ship's sick bay, where he could quickly receive everything she needed.

When the elevator door slid shut, she kicked off her high heeled shoes, snatched them from the floor, hiked up her long dress and sprinted toward the room. With her card key in her free hand, she swiped twice before the door lock flashed green. Inside the cabin, she collapsed against the wall panting. Her pulse raced. With no time to waste, she pushed off the wall and mentally categorized the things she needed to do.

Fifteen minutes would be plenty of time to grab the things she needed, including the inflatable boat she'd purchased last summer. Her original plan had been to jump off the balcony, but the distance to the water terrified her.

As she'd unpacked, she'd studied the floorplan of the ship and discovered she could take a back stairway to a lower floor and go over the rail. In the dry suit that covered her from head to toe she'd be unrecognizable. Once in the water the dark ocean would make her hard to spot. She'd studied the maps and memorized the entire route. Her clothing re-hung in the closet was indistinguishable from other similar dresses. When the investigators came, her husband wouldn't be able to say what she'd had worn.

She wiggled into the form-fitting dry suit before grabbing the packed nylon duffle with the waterproof insert from under the bed. .

The ship shuddered followed by a loud, long bang, then lurched, tossing her to the floor.

Her ribs screamed in pain. Nicole bit her lips to keep from crying out. Blood pounded in her veins and pulsed in her ears. She grabbed the bed's leg and pulled herself up, using the furniture as leverage to stand, mentally examining each joint and limb for injury. Outside the sliding glass door, lights flickered on nearby land.

She blinked. Shouldn't she be staring at the Mediterranean? Moving closer, the dim outline of an island appeared out of the darkness. The ship was close enough for her to identify a lighthouse and electric lights burning in the windows of homes lining the coast.

She tugged on the patio doors. The slight tilt of the ship interfered with the easy workings. Raising her leg, she braced her foot against the jam and pulled with all her might. The door gave an inch at a time until it opened far enough she could slip out. A fierce gust of wind assaulted her. She clung to the balcony rail.

The ship's interior lights flashed and the vessel which had been lit up like Christmas tree went black.

In the darkness she found clarity.

The ship jerked and seized, throwing her to the deck. Unseen voices, streaked with panic rose in a variety of languages. There had been no life boat drill, but a sane person would be donning an orange vest and heading toward a rescue station.

An announcement blared through the

intercom in the hallway. A calm accented voice assured passengers that the electrical problem was being fixed. There was no need for panic.

Were they kidding? An electrical problem didn't sound like a can opener ripping through metal. Nor did it cause a ship of this size to behave like an inebriated spectator at a rock and roll concert.

She hadn't planned to take the life vest. Now she crawled across the floor to the closet, pulled herself up and yanked one from the top shelf. The lights came on while she was sliding it over her head.

With light she could open the safe. The boat lurched again. The floor slanted, but Nicole widened her stance and quickly entered the combination she'd set earlier in the day.

Her initial plan had been to leave items in the safe, particularly her jewelry so it wouldn't look like she'd run. But if this ship was going down, she might as well take it all.

She scraped everything into another waterproof bag and added it to her growing pile. Using furniture to keep herself upright, she checked the view again and was dismayed. The angle was such that she no longer saw the island, but the churning dark sea water.

Time moved quickly. Her husband cover arrive at any minute. With the slope of the ship he'd want his life vest. At the very least he'd sent Gunter. She crammed her hair under the rubber cap, grabbed her bag, the folded boat and wiggled through the door onto the deck.

Death was foremost on her mind, but she dismissed it, choosing instead to focus on life, freedom and escape. Squeezing her eyes shut, she inhaled a deep breath and climbed onto the rail.

*She could do this.*

*There were no other choices.*

The ship rocked. She forced her hand to let go, uttering a small prayer for Libby's safety, she leapt from the boat into the freezing water.

The shock to her system was so great that it was all she could do to hold on to her possessions as her body was buffeted about under water. When her head remerged, she gulped air. Her teeth chattered.

Even in the dry suit the water chilled her skin. The ship loomed above her, she kicked hard and half-swam, half-dog paddled until she reached a patch of moonlight on the water. Her muscles were stiff but after a minute of fumbling, she found the inflated boat's cord and gave it a hard tug before scrambling aboard. Lying face down, panting more from fear than exertion, she heard nothing but the waves slapping the raft's sides.

Time and fear were her enemy. She struggled to sit up and position the oars. The immense ship wobbled, then went dark again. Screams filled the air, urging her into faster action. Her first thought was to row for the closest land, but a sinking ship dictated the passengers would require evacuation to the very island in front of her. What good was her escape if her husband immediately followed?

Could the ship right itself?

Life boats would be lowered in a matter of minutes. No matter where she looked her only option was water, but she'd studied the route. This had to be the Tyrrhenian Sea which meant somewhere across the inky sea Italy was at her back.

If she rowed for the mainland the strong wind would fight her every step of the way. It would be the harder path, but one her husband would discount, believing her to be incapable of such a feat. It was the one thing that would persuade him she was dead, because if he thought, even for an instant that she was alive, she'd never be safe.

But her drowning, real or fictional, would have a lasting effect. No reporter, even a politically-biased one, would believe any man could have three wives who died from drowning. The spotlight would raise doubts. At worst, the next few months would be awkward. At best, Linus would be removed from office or forced to resign.

*Forward push, backward pull.* She recited the chant she'd used on the rowing machine in Linus' exercise room. *Forward push, backward pull.*

She'd rowed for several minutes when the red and white emergency lights came on highlighting the ship's outline. She'd covered more distance than she'd imagined. Still no lifeboats were being detached. Had she misread the situation?

The ship tilted precariously. Sounds travel over the water, but she heard nothing. The cruise ship was drifting out to sea. Why weren't the passengers being evacuated?

For a brief moment she worried. Linus and the guards were in danger. Then the black humor struck her. Wouldn't it be funny if Linus drowned and she was the one who lived? She brushed back the tears that ran down her cheeks.

*Forward push, backward pull.*

She firmed her jaw and ignored the pain in her ribs as she continued to row, hoping that she hadn't misjudged their location and the Italian coastline was indeed somewhere behind her.

*Forward push, backward pull.*

It was so much harder than she'd imagine.

At home she would rest when she tired, drink water. Here nothing respite. Doggedly she carried on.

Hours later, smaller boats churned up waves as they moved at a fast clip toward the area where the ship had last been before the lights had shut down completely. The wake battered her causing her to drift in the wrong direction, but she avoided getting close enough to be seen.

*Forward push, backward pull.*

She rowed, then rested, then rowed again while singing songs from her childhood to keep her mind off her aches and pains and keep her spirits from sinking. Quitting beckoned. It would be so easy to just let go, but she refused.

*Forward push, backward pull.*

Gloves protected her hands from blisters, but still they ached. The stiff rubber suit chafed. Quitting beckoned. It would be so easy to just let go. She longed to drop the oars, slip over the edge of the boat and let the water take her troubles away, but couldn't. Beth had chosen that way out. Nicole had always been the strong one.

The silent vow she'd made at her sister's funeral was to care for her daughter and she intended to keep her word. Stopping was not an option, so she continued through the sweat, the tears and the pain.

*Forward push, backward pull.*

Finally, when she thought she couldn't go on, streaks of sunlight shot through the trees heralding a new day. Her exhaustion was so complete that it took several minutes for the realization to hit − trees meant land. And land meant she wasn't going to die at sea.

# Chapter Four

*Monday, January 16th*
*Portland, Oregon*

Austin Stevens stared at the gray Willamette River through the floor-to-ceiling windows of their new luxurious office. Rain trickled down the windows. The overcast sky was as gloomy as his mood. Most of the trees he saw below were stripped of leaves.

Traffic on the nearby Burnside Bridge moved at a crawl and even the homeless, so prevalent in the downtown area, weren't tackling the elements.

To the outside world this twenty-third floor view represented status. Most executives who sought the services of Stevens' Security were comforted by the rich appointments and peaceful colors chosen by a decorator. Men who came to see them were anxious.

Austin spent more days behind his computer than any of the other six field agents. Only the support staff manned the desks on a daily basis. His cyber training, internet knowledge and tracking ability combined with

Travis's planning and assessment skills had made their fledging company, now only four years old, a serious player in an overcrowded field.

Today, Austin was restless. The back of his neck prickled. Had he forgotten something important? If so, he had no idea what. He'd checked his calendar and email and found nothing, but still he couldn't settle into the routine of work.

He ran a hand over his two day-old beard, mentally revisiting his current cases. Unable to sit, he paced the twelve-by-fourteen office until he couldn't take one more minute of soothing gray carpeting.

He had to get out of there. The gym was three blocks away, but punching a bag or lifting weights would key him up. He pulled a pair of shorts out of a drawer allotted to work-out gear and grabbed some running shoes.

On the twenty-third floor of an executive building no one used the stairs. Shirtless, he stretched, easing his tense muscles before he pounded up seven flights and down thirty-one.

By the time he was on his second return trip, sweat dripped from his chest and back, he'd unwound enough to think. If work wasn't the problem, then it had to be his brothers.

Travis was blissful. While he hadn't

persuaded his mystery writer, Abigail to marry him, he appeared for the first time in his life to be content. Austin was happy for him. But marriage and children weren't in his dreams.

His footsteps slowed as he finally stopped to catch his breath on the upward trek.

Their childhood had been a nightmare he wouldn't wish on his worst enemy. At best his father had been a bully. At worst, drugs had changed him into a monster. He'd beaten his wife and terrorized his sons.

Austin shook his head, water from his scalp sprinkled the concrete.

He'd passed his childhood years as a stuttering and stammering nerd, hiding behind a computer monitor or in the pages of books. Poverty was a constant reminder of their status. The last neighborhood was so dismal his older brother had been forced into a gang in order to survive.

Austin thought it couldn't get any worse until the day he spotted his father's battered pickup following the school bus on the home route. He convinced Travis to leave the bus early and they walked six miles home in a circuitous route. Both knew it was just a matter of time before the family would move again in the middle of the night. For Austin, it had been the final straw that changed him. No longer was he content to sit back and let life impact him. From the age of eleven on, he'd tackled life with everything he possessed. His survival and that of his family had depended upon it.

Middle School had been a baptismal in pain. He and Travis were in different schools for the first time. He'd gotten his height much later than his brother, but he'd learned that a small kid in a new school meant daily fights. Austin could take a beating. When other boys discovered he wouldn't back down, the odds changed. No longer was it one-on-one.

Five boys surrounded him behind the bleachers. He was about to get his teeth kicked in when tall, burly Sam Sampson joined the group. The others crowed in delight.

With a grin, Sam punched the one closest to him and stretched out a leg to kick another. Austin was stunned. He had an ally. Gleefully, he jumped into the fray.

That day had forged the bonds of brotherhood - taking on a Stevens meant taking on Sampson. They'd eaten dinner together last night. Sam hadn't been unhappy.

He'd reached his floor and stopped to rest his forehead against the stairwell's cool concrete wall, sorry he'd dredged up the past, but pretty sure whatever bothered him had nothing to do with Sam or Travis.

He trusted his instincts. Something was going down and it wasn't going to be good.

The door opened, and Travis, his expression grim, stepped into the stairwell. Inwardly Austin braced himself.

"You need a shower."

Austin sniffed the air. "Thought I'd grab one at the gym I'm just picking up clothes.

Travis shook his head. "No time. We need to talk."

Austin's scalp tingled, a sure signal of danger. "Sure."

He folded his arms across his chest and leaned against the door jamb, hoping his casual pose would persuade his brain that everything was okay. "What's going on?"

"Senator Layton's wife, the blonde we met last week who refused our help… "

Every nerve in his body went on red alert. She'd been in trouble. Why hadn't he gone back to see her? Why hadn't he protected her? He'd waited for her to call but she hadn't. He'd been a fool not to go after her. He forced himself to speak the words stuck in his throat, "Is she dead?"

Travis paused. His brother never spoke without thinking. He lacked the impulsive gene Austin had sought to control all his life. But there were times like right now when those pauses made him crazy.

"Yes," he urged, hoping against hope that his brother wasn't about to deliver devastating news.

"Missing."

Austin exhaled a pent-up breath, but couldn't loosen the tightness in his chest. Missing was better than dead. Missing meant hope and possibilities. His body tensed the way it did when he was about to go wheels-up on a mission. Travis wouldn't be telling him this unless they were being called to action.

His instincts took over and before he knew it, he sat in front of his desk with his brother looking over his shoulder. Finding people was what he did best. He placed his fingers on the keyboard ready to type search information. "What do you know?"

"That Italian ship in the news last week – the one that went down in the Mediterranean on Friday she was on it."

His wrists dropped from the keyboard. "What?"

His response produced a half-smile from his brother. "The ship flipped over. She was not among the passengers who've been found." He swung his body into a cushioned chair in front of the desk.

"Start at the beginning. Tell me everything."

Travis glanced at the papers in his hand. "The Senator and his wife were at dinner. She left with one of two men from the security detail. That man was later found drowned, trapped in an elevator underwater on one of the lower floors. According to Layton the man, a Joaquin Alvarez – was supposed to be with his wife. He had no reason to be in belly of the ship unless the elevator plummeted from an upper floor – which is the theory being put forth. However, there is no evidence to support it."

"Where did you get this information?"

"Insurance company. Layton requested paperwork to file a death claim."

Austin leapt out of his chair paced to the window and back. "You're kidding, right? This is Monday morning. What is he doing even back in the states, much less filing a death claim?"

"Mourning." His brother's dry tone helped Austin marginally relax. "The insurance company is livid. This is the Senator's third multi-million-dollar claim against them – all for wives who died in drowning incidents."

"What? How?"

"Bathtub, swimming pool, Mediterranean Sea. The insurance company needs us to verify her death and determine its cause."

Austin read between the lines as well as anyone. He leaned over the chair clutching the armrests. "They think the husband killed her? Three wives drowned? Jeez, is he the world's stupidest criminal or so arrogant he believes he's above the law?"

"The company is being careful. What they are saying is that a widower three times over is statistically unlikely – particularly when each wife was well insured – and the cause of death is the same."

Mentally Austin raised his eyebrows. He templed his fingers, as his mind ordered the sequence of things to be done. "Let's expand our investigation to include similarities with previous circumstances. He's short a guard. Send Tyrone to Illinois. We'll provide a cover story, but get him hired. We may need a man on the inside."

Travis nodded. "Let's investigate how Mrs. Layton spent her days especially the past two weeks."

"I did a little checking on her, trying to figure out what her husband held over her. She's got an institutionalized niece. Brain damaged from a car wreck that killed the mother. Found it interesting that the child was in San Diego instead of Illinois. However, a little backtracking revealed that Nicole moved the girl six times in the past three years, each location further from her home. What do you think that means?"

"Good question. I'll find out." Travis jotted another note on his paper. "Now, about Mrs. Layton's disappearance what's your gut telling you?"

"That she's running for her life. I'm leaving for Italy as fast as I can get to the airport."

Travis rose from the chair, a wealth of understanding in his eyes. "If she's alive, you'll find her."

Austin hoped his brother was correct and he wasn't too late.

# Chapter Five

*Monday, January 16th*
*Washington, DC*

Hiram Lynch, CEO of Black Adder, a paramilitary government contractor, leaned back in his leather chair, folded his arms across his chest, and stared at the acoustic tile ceiling. He loved the company he'd slaved night and day to create. Luck had never been a factor. People made their own luck, but today promised to be an excellent day. One hand sought the worry stone in his pocket. As always he found comfort in the worn groove.

Linus Layton, the highest ranking senator on the Appropriations Committee was in trouble. Hiram had made an extraordinary living out of rescuing those in the beltway from real-world consequences. In turn he'd been awarded numerous government security contracts. Cleaning up after this man could be very lucrative because the one thing he knew for certain, the Senator wasn't telling him the entire truth. And Black Adder was in the truth-finding business.

Layton's young, beautiful wife was missing,

presumed drowned when the ship on which she sailed went down due to captain error. No evidence indicated sabotage. The Senator claimed to be frantic with worry.

Although a man frantic with worry wouldn't have flown home the morning after the accident while bodies were still being recovered. And Hiram didn't discount the undertone of anger in Layton's voice.

What was the man failing to tell him? That would be worth discovering.

Hiram gathered photos of the six-man team he'd chosen to find her. Three were from one of his Strike Force teams. Jones, Cartwright, and Snyder – two divers and a tracker. Getting them to Italy as soon as possible meant splitting teams and robbing other jobs of personnel, but Layton's retainer alone would make it worth his time.

The fourth man, Reichert was in Switzerland. The greedy bastard would fight being pulled off the Secret Service job, but Reichert, unlike many of his agents, did not tiptoe around. He operated to the point and never backed down. If someone had personal information, Reichert would ferret it out.

Black Adder had agents in Eastern Europe and others in Afghanistan who could be in Rome in a matter of hours. Hiram chose the remaining members of the team with deliberation, selecting skills over personalities.

Jones and Cartwright needed to get in the water immediately. If the woman was trapped in her cabin where her husband indicated she was supposed to have been, the issue of finding her would be mute.

But if she wasn't…

Reichert, Snyder and Wildman Beastly could cover the surrounding land. The three would be more than enough to find her. People in hiding underestimated how hard it was to go to the ground. Inevitably they left a trail. Sooner or later everybody was found.

His last choice was the hardest. He hoped he wasn't misreading Layton's cryptic message. "I want to know how she died."

Hiram had purposefully treaded carefully in an effort to determine the other man's intent. "If she's still alive?"

"She won't be." The Senator's voice had been resolute. "I'm sure you'll discover she died in a tragic accident."

He didn't want her found? "On land?"

"Am I putting my faith in the wrong man? Don't disappoint me."

Black Adder did not specialize in murder for hire, but sometimes exceptions had to be made – particularly for a man with power and connections.

His last choice was Charles "Laser-Beam" Ernst, sniper.

Hiram searched the internet for multiple photos of the missing woman. She was exquisite, the type of beauty who unconsciously drew a man's attention. Hiding would be difficult. Men could smell a desperate woman.

He pursed his lips. Since Layton hadn't been forthcoming with the facts perhaps he had no clue as to how deceptive a woman could be. Why would a woman trained from birth to marry well leave a wealthy, powerful husband? Most would have hired the best divorce lawyer they could find. Usually when a wife disappeared it was because the husband had decided to rid himself of her. He didn't hire a team to find out how she died.

Hiram tilted his head to gaze at the ceiling, feeling the brush of his long hair under his collar. Secrets. He loved them. They had made him rich.

A beautiful woman could get a man to do anything. She wouldn't be without a protector for long. He scratched his cheek. In fact, she might have had someone in the wings. Could be worthwhile to see who else was hunting for her. He punched a number on his cell phone. When the automated line answered he added a code.

Immediately a female voice answered, asking politely, "What can I do for you?"

"I need passenger lists to and from Rome on every flight for the past seventy-two hours and let's keep running it throughout the week."

"I'll email it in a few moments."

Hiram smiled and sat back in his chair. It was only January. This was an omen. It was going to be a very good year.

◈

*Porto Santa Stefano, Tuscany*

Blinding sunlight burst through the tall windows lining the dormitory room of the youth hostel like a cosmic explosion. Every muscle group protested as Nicole shifted her aching body on the thin, single sheet-less mattress. An involuntary groan escaped. Automatically, she clamped her lips together and lifted her head to see who heard.

"Well, you're awake."

As she struggled to sit, Nicole shifted her head into the shadows and blinked. On the adjacent bed in the youth hostel were two women, girls really, both early twenties, casually dressed in jeans and t-shirts.

"The owners of this fine establishment..." The brunette's tone reeked of sarcasm as she waved her skinny tattooed arm toward the white-on-white walls, sending the blue feathers braided into her hair aflutter. "… believed you were dead."

A second girl, curled into a ball at the end of the bed, sobbed, her eyes swollen and her nose red.

Nicole opened her mouth to answer, but only the hacking sound of disuse came from her throat. She moistened her dry cracked lips with her tongue. The brunette tossed a half-finished bottle of water.

When Nicole's hand automatically reached out and snagged it from the air, instant pain ran up her arm. She glanced at her blistered hands and shuddered, imagining what they would have looked like if she hadn't worn gloves.

Holding the bottle by her fingertips, she hesitated briefly before her thirst won out over her mother's belief that one did not drink from the same container as strangers.

The tepid liquid soothed her parched throat and she could've emptied the bottle, but politeness dictated she leave some. Reluctantly she thrust the bottle toward the brunette who threw up her hands, refusing to take it.

"Finish it. You need it more than I do."

"Thanks." Nicole tilted the bottle and gulped the remainder, before slumping against the wall.

A loud sob was emitted by the blonde.

"We'll figure it out, Kaitlyn." The brunette's words were meant to soothe, but her tone was one of disinterest. "You're not the only one with problems."

Nicole eyed the brunette who sized her up in return. "What's wrong with her?" she asked to keep from being plied with questions.

"We took one of the tour boats to see the cruise ship that sank. Katie dropped her wallet overboard and lost all her money. Not that there was that much left." The girls exchanged an accusatory look each holding the other to blame. "Our plane leaves in two days. We've got to get back to Rome, and we're tapped out."

Panic raced from her stomach to her throat. "A cruise ship sank? What happened?"

"According to the news, the captain was showing off, sailed too close to an island and hit rocks. The good news is not too many people died."

Exactly how many was 'not too many'? But Nicole kept her thoughts to herself.

"Anyway, the captain left the ship before everyone was off, so he's in big trouble." The brunette tossed her a copy of an Italian newspaper featuring a large photo of the *Costa Concordia* lying on its side.

Nicole schooled her face to hide her shock.

"I thought you said it sank."

"That's what everyone is calling it."

"When did this happen?" She strove for calm disinterest when she wanted to quiz both girls for every detail they knew.

"Friday night."

Definitely her ship. How many dead? How many missing? She squinted and scanned the words trying to translate the Italian words into Spanish without much success. The bright sunlight gave her a headache.

How much time had she lost? "What day is it?"

"Monday. You've slept for almost two days."

Her mind raced to come up with an explanation. "The doctor changed my medication. I must have had a bad reaction. I feel like I've been run over by a truck."

Both girls snickered, accepting the lie, but it was Kaitlyn who said, "You kind of look like it, too."

Nicole automatically reached up to smooth her hair and felt the tangles. She glanced around the room with its sterile walls and rows of orderly beds. Only one other bed was occupied at the far end of the room. The sleeping form appeared to be a young man, but she wasn't certain.

How could she have slept for so long? She had to locate an English newspaper or a television and find out everything about the accident. Careful not to appear too interested, she studied the two girls. Had Linus looked for her?

She took a deep breath and forced herself to relax. Panic would not help, and the one thing she knew for certain was that her husband hadn't found her yet.

Her raft had crashed against the shore near enough to see the outlines of buildings. She had dragged the boat onto land, but had been too exhausted to go one step further.

Safe for the first time in hours, she'd slept using the boat for a bed until mid-day and then stashed it under a tree along with her life jacket and dry suit. It was possible her only means of escape would be on the sea, so instead of deflating the boat, she covered it with branches, leaves and debris.

She'd passed two *pensiones* before deciding the youth hostel looked like the best bet for a traveler lacking ID. She'd jammed a baseball cap over her hair and concocted a story about a boyfriend who stole her purse. The overweight man behind the desk offered no sympathy until she flashed two hundred dollar bills. Sure she'd overpaid, she'd crawled into bed using her lumpy suitcase for a pillow and fallen asleep.

The traveling girls' casual look was one Nicole longed to emulate, but she'd played the rich, proper wife so long she'd lost the ability. Her clothes were too new and too well matched. Kaitlyn was close to her size. Two backpacks leaned against the bed. One proudly displayed a Canadian flag.

"Where's home?" Nicole asked.

"Vancouver, BC. You?"

*Where was she from? Why hadn't she come up with a cover story?*

"Sweetwater Lake, Louisiana." Her first instinct on hearing her words was to slap a hand over her mouth. Her painful past surged to the forefront.

Nicole busied herself digging through her bag for a comb and struggling for control.

Merely by saying the words she'd drudged up a memory she'd trained years to forget. As clearly as if she was standing in the backyard that bordered a lake, she could smell the new mowed grass and hear crickets at the water's edge. Fire flies danced on the night air. Sweetwater Lake had been her first home. An idyllic childhood, the kind of small town life that television shows like Mayberry RFD had tried to reinvent. It had been perfect.

Until the summer night her world had

crashed. The sheriff's patrol car sat in the driveway flashing red and blue lights. Nosy neighbors with folded arms and forbidding expressions stood on their lawns. Her beloved father, a man of a thousand silly games, knelt beside the patrol car, handcuffed with head bowed.

Her mother on her knees in the doorway screamed and cried and beseeched the heavens. Beth huddled next to her, bawling loudly, tears streaming down her cheeks.

All Nicole could remember thinking was that there must have been a mistake. Her father could never do anything wrong.

Despite her belief, he went to jail.

After a while, her mother and new stepfather carefully scrubbed him from their lives, leaving nothing to connect them.

Except he must have known, because once he got out of prison, he moved nearby. Immediately he contacted his daughters and begged them to visit. She'd never gone, but Beth had. Nicole had read the trial transcripts. She'd learned the kind of man her father was. She didn't need to locate him, the sexual predator web site posted his name, age, and address for all to see.

She shook her head. Now was not the time to rehash those memories. "Whose backpack is this?" She pointed toward the one decorated with the flag.

Kaitlyn craned her head to look over her shoulder. "Mine."

Her lips worked before her mind could assess the plan. "I can give you enough money to get home, but I need you to trade bags and clothes with me."

Both girls instantly lost their easy demeanor. "Why?" Skepticism etched Kaitlyn's features.

Nicole took a deep breath. "It doesn't matter. You have secrets and so do I, but you need money and I need to look like someone else."

Surprisingly it was the brunette who seemed to accept the situation without questions. She nodded toward the blonde. "Take off your clothes."

Nicole glanced around the room. "Here?"

"Sure. That guy's dead to the world, and the bathroom is tiny and stinks like shit."

Reluctantly Nicole fingered the top button of her shirt as Kaitlyn tugged her t-shirt over her head and unfastened her jeans. She had to go through with it. Now was not the time to lose her nerve.

But it wasn't until she removed her shirt that she remembered the ace bandage that bound her chest. The bruises on her arms had faded. Only a couple of places had tinges of yellow-green. She stood to shuck her slacks.

The brunette let out a low whistle. "He sure did a number on you."

"It's not what you think." Her automatic defense sprung to her lips. Her cheeks warmed in embarrassment. "No. That's wrong. It's exactly what you think."

"What's your name?"

Here was the time for honesty, but Nicole wasn't quite there. "Lynn," She said, giving her middle name instead.

"I'm Valerie. If you're really going to do this, you need a cut and color. I'm in beauty school. If you let me, I can help."

Nicole blinked back the tears that threatened to spill down her cheeks. "Thank you."

# Chapter Six

*Rome, Italy*
*Tuesday, January 17th*

With heightened senses, Austin swept through the Custom's door, tossing his overnight bag over one shoulder. Being on foreign soil always made him alert, but this time something foreboding hung in the air adding extra caution to his step.

Without appearing too interested he surveyed the surrounding crowd. Several passengers had disembarked from his flight and like him pressed toward the exits. Waiting outside the double doors were a sea of faces, many holding signs. Years of surveillance work had him scanning the edges until he saw them.

Unlike him they hadn't felt the need to be discreet. Austin had worked to shuck his military appearance, but these men hadn't, and in this part of the world that meant they might still be employed in quasi-military ventures. Their gazes shifted from their cell phones to the crowd searching for a match for whatever photos their phones had produced.

He slumped to hide his height and turned his foot, adding a deformity as he shuffled along the crowd. He sensed rather than saw one of the men kick off from the wall. At the first opening available, he shuffled into an alcove that housed a bathroom. Instead of continuing, he crouched as other pushed by him. His fingers touched his shoes as though he meant to retie his laceless loafers.

Sure enough, he'd picked up a tail. The man leaned against the far wall.

Interesting. The fact that he was being watched cheered him immensely. Now they were getting somewhere. There was a good chance someone thought she was still alive. Then he sobered. He didn't have time to waste. The race was on to find her before others did.

He needed privacy for his next move. Grabbing his bag, he headed to a bathroom stall to text Travis about the latest development. Once done, Austin replaced his denim jacket with a sport coat, artistically draped a scarf around his neck, added horn rim glasses, a mustache and a goatee. He exchanged the ball cap for a beret. Being a good hunter meant being invisible and he'd come prepared.

The man hired to tail him didn't even glance his direction when he sailed by, freeing him to locate the helo he'd hired to take him to Giglio

Island. If these men were who he thought he'd pick them up again when he started asking questions about the ship.

Like everyone, he'd seen the news articles that showed pictures of the large cruise ship partially submerged in water, but the photos didn't do the scene justice. A quick overview told him how lucky the Italian line had been that the ship hadn't lost more passengers. By all accounts, the evacuation had been chaotic and disorganized.

According to Travis's report, the body guard had thrown the Senator overboard, jumped in after him, and gotten them both safely to shore.

Austin snorted. If he had a wife who was missing he wouldn't have left without her. And neither would his brother. In fact, Travis would have dismantled the ship if Abigail was missing. Austin smiled despite his concerns. Knowing Abby she would have been the one who'd taken charge of the evacuation and brought order to chaos.

Landing on the island hadn't been a mistake, but no one was glad to see him. The two Italian officials were crammed into a tiny room decorated with navigational maps. His saving grace was his ability to speak flawless Italian. The Navy had taught him many skills, but it was the SEALs that had forced him to master languages.

The investigators who greeted him wore a polite, but harried smile. Every question he asked was answered but with reserve. Had he spoken English, he was sure the men wouldn't have answered.

The mid-fiftyish man who spoke, made it clear Austin had not been the first to waste his time with questions.

"Who else has been here?"

"The American Senator hired outsiders to locate his wife's body." The cool demeanor and hard black eyes did not welcome additional inquiries and the second investigator ignored them by turning his attention to the paperwork on his desk.

Austin sympathized, but needed answers. "The Americans – how did they think they could find the answers before you?"

The black eyes snapped and the man's mouth narrowed. "Without permission, they had divers search the ship before ours arrived."

Austin's face must have shown surprise because the official nodded and felt the sudden need to justify how that had been to happen.

"Had the Captain been honest about what happened, we could have saved time and gotten our divers in first. But the Americans were so aggressive. Speaking louder is the same as having a translator. The island people are unsophisticated, not deaf."

He threw up his hands, agitated. "Quizzing all the locals, showing photographs, flashing cash. They interfered with us at every turn. It took the police to get them to leave."

Austin played dumb. "Why did they think the locals would know something?"

"The woman is missing. Her body has not been recovered." He said, pointing out the obvious.

Who else was hunting her? And who could have been organized to get their divers in the water so quickly?

Only one American name came to mind. Black Adder.

Austin was sure if Nicole's body had been found, he wouldn't have seen the men at the airport. Weariness lined the official's features. The news reported less than thirty died. But these men had viewed each body. Thirty was more deaths than most ever saw.

"If she drowned, eventually her body will be discovered, trapped in another part of the ship or will wash up on shore." His tone was resigned. Obviously, he thought she was dead.

Austin studied the wall map with the magnetic flags showing the ship's path. It hit the rocks, ripping open the underside. Water poured in, but the ship's momentum pushed the vessel further out to sea. Then the arrows showed backtracking.

"What happened here that forced the ship back toward the island?" He pointed to the map.

"Wind. Thirty knots per hour. Drove the ship back. If the ship had sunk here," the short official pointed to edge of the arrows, "thousands would have died. God works in mysterious ways."

Austin thanked the men and headed toward the lighthouse that overlooked the island and the beached vessel almost completely submerged due to the high tide. He gazed out to sea and tried to visualize Nicole's thought processes. What would a woman do if tossed into the sea? Assuming Layton hadn't beaten her first.

If she'd made it to the island she would have been spotted. The locals had no loyalty to protect her. Hyperthermia would have set in if she'd swam. Rescue boats would have been risky. She was beautiful woman – hard to miss. Someone would have talked. Layton would have made it worth their while. The officials had already confirmed money had been offered in exchange for information.

If she drowned it was possible her body might never be recovered. Which begged the question – why was Black Adder hunting for her? Only one person could have hired them – the grieving husband.

No doubt he had stood on this exact spot, weighed all the possibilities, yet still believed his wife wasn't dead. Why? If he'd killed her or attempted it, he wouldn't have hired an expensive search team. Black Adder had an inflated view of their own worth.

Nothing made sense.

Sir Arthur Conan Doyle once wrote, "When you have eliminated the impossible, whatever remains, however improbable, must be the truth."

Austin's next step was obvious. He headed to the helo.

His pilot flew low, skirting the Tuscan coast line. With powerful binoculars Austin scanned the trees, looking for anything out of place. "Wait. Circle back."

If it had been darker, he might have missed the gray object under the tree. "Find a place to land."

The pilot landed about two klicks from the area. Austin raced back searching the gravel roadway for a clue to her presence.

The boat had been covered, but not well enough. It hadn't been deflated. A mistake. The small dry suit he found tucked under the oars indicated the owner had been a teen or female. The cap contained a few long blonde hairs. But it was lifejacket bearing the ship's name that convinced him that Nicole had gotten this far.

With a knife he punctured the boat, dug a hole further in the woods and buried the evidence of the boat, life vest and dry suit. No doubt she believed she might have to use it again. Instead it served as a signpost to announce her presence. If he found it others would, too.

He stared at the sea. Where would she have gotten a raft? The manufacturer's tag indicated it was American-made. A dry-suit that fit.

His smile had him grinning like a fool. Nicole Layton hadn't needed his help because she'd already planned to escape. All she'd done was take advance of an opportunity. Oh, man. This woman was smart. And determined. Not many women, or for that matter men would have rowed as far as she did against those head winds.

But if she'd been foresighted enough to bring an inflatable raft, she might have left clues behind. No wonder the Senator thought she was alive. Austin marveled at the will power it had taken her to get here. His admiration for her grew.

When he'd insisted upon warning her, it had

been wasted breath. She already knew the dangers. She lived them. The child had been the mitigating factor. She couldn't leave because her husband would go to any extreme to force her compliance.

His mother had been brave when she'd left her husband and taken both boys, but she'd run in fear, directionless. To protect the family, Travis and Austin had learned to strategize their moves.

Nicole had no one. Austin studied the topography, trying to determine which direction an exhausted woman might head. Uphill if she was smart, downhill if she was too tired to think clearly. He went with his gut and headed downhill to the nearby town of Port Santa Stefano.

# Chapter Seven

*Tuesday, January 17th*
*Washington DC*

Hiram Lynch held his annoyance in check as he hit re-dial to connect to Senator Layton's personal cell. His fingers dug for the worry stone in his pocket. Layton remained cloistered at his Lake Forest home, giving an elegant appearance to his suffering which Hiram knew to be a lie.

On the fifth ring Layton answered. After the customary greetings, and a rambling diatribe on the recent winter storm that dumped twelve inches of snow on the north shore of Lake Michigan, the Senator, without waiting for a response, asked the question he could no longer contain. "So, have you found her?" The underlying edge of eagerness belied his public sense of loss.

Hiram's shoulders tensed as they got to the meat of the matter. "Not yet. What makes you think she's alive?"

A long pause followed. Hiram's thumb rubbed the stone. After all the years he'd sought solace from it, he was surprised he hadn't smoothed away the artificial indention. Days like this gave the stone a workout.

"Money is missing from my safe."

Even knowing Layton couldn't see his gesture, Hiram nodded. He'd figured she'd done something telling that prevented him from accepting her death. "How much?" he asked, wishing they were having this discussion in person. Non-verbal clues revealed more honest answers than words. He guessed high. "A million dollars?"

"Of course not." The indignation in his voice convinced Hiram he was telling the truth. "I don't keep that kind of money in my house safe."

Hiram waited. Finally the silence got to the other man. "Around a hundred thousand."

Hiram choked back his surprise. He'd expected a figure in the ten-to-twenty thousand range. What was a man like Layton doing with a hundred thousand dollars lying around? Millionaires had infinite tax shelters and secret oversees accounts for spare change. People who needed large amounts of cash on hand tended to operate on the shady side of the law. Layton would bear watching.

"When did it go missing?"

"A few days before we left for Italy, Nicole insisted upon visiting her institutionalized niece in San Diego. She wanted to move her to yet another facility. My God, man she's moved that child fourteen times in the past three years."

Hiram didn't want to get into the specifics of a family quarrel, but he'd researched the situation enough to know she had moved the girl six times, not the fourteen the Senator claimed.

"You refused?" Hiram asked, knowing the answer ahead of time.

"She didn't need to move that child again."

Hiram felt a pang of sorrow for his wife and for the little girl whose only name seemed to be 'that child'. "Are you sure she took the money? "

"The safe has a camera." Layton gloated as though he'd thwarted a master criminal.

Tantalizing questions crowded Hiram's mind. "She had the combination?"

"Apparently. Although I didn't give it to her." The sulky answer came through the receiver.

*Interesting.* "How'd she get it?"

"No idea. Only my father and I know the combination. I never opened the safe with her in the room."

Hiram's fingers tightened around the stone. Slowly he uncurled them and drew his hand out of his pocket. Either the Senator was lying or Nicole Layton was a lot smarter than her husband knew. Lynch suspected the latter. But the answer didn't matter. If the Senator was lying, he wasn't about to reveal the truth now.

"So where's the child?"

Another long drawn out pause confirmed another supposition. His wife had needed the money to move the girl and the Senator had no clue where. Rather than wait for the other man to put a spin on the details, Hiram asked, "Was your wife traveling alone?"

"No. A bodyguard was with her."

He made a mental note to run a background check on the Senator's household staff and guards. "The one I met?"

"Yes."

Hiram stared at the ceiling for several minutes. "Do you need me to interview him?"

"Not yet."

So he'd considered the idea and eliminated it. Why?

He hadn't a doubt that a beautiful woman like Nicole Layton could find someone to help her. The question was who? Was it the bumbling guard, who among other duties shined Layton's shoes, or Austin Stevens, who'd taken a last minute Monday night flight to Rome? "How do you know Stevens Security?"

He gritted his teeth as he listened to a voice in the background and a muffled reply from the Senator.

"Who?" Layton asked.

"Stevens Security out of Portland, Oregon," Hiram said slowly, emphasizing each word.

"Oh, them. Gave me a quote on a home security system." Layton's dismissive tone caught Hiram's attention. "Didn't hire them, though. The younger brother is gay."

While he used the politically correct term, Hiram suspected it was not the word the Senator preferred, but regardless of the terminology, the hair on Hiram's arms stood up. "What makes you say that?"

Layton snorted. "Openly flirted with my guard. Freaked the hell out of Gunter."

Trying to ease the headache pound behind his eyeballs, Hiram rubbed his forehead. Civilians could be such idiots. "Was Stevens ever alone with your wife?"

"Alone? Of course not." Another telling pause followed. "Well, he wanted to see the Heads of State collection of place settings." Layton's tone edged with annoyance. "They were together no more than a few minutes."

Hiram closed his eyes and inhaled deeply to maintain his calm. What freaking security specialist wanted to see the dishes? Didn't that raise a fucking red flag the size of Arizona for God's sake? No wonder the guy was in trouble.

When the silence lengthened, the Senator asked, "Why?"

"Because Austin Stevens landed in Rome six hours ago. I'm trying to figure out if your wife called him or he was hired by someone else."

"Don't be ridiculous. Why would she call him?"

"Maybe they made a connection."

The Senator's belly laugh might have been refreshing if Hiram hadn't been so convinced Stevens's appearance was not coincidental.

"Nicole was one damned cold fish. Wanted a meal ticket, not a real man. Doubt if a security guard's bank balance would entice her."

Layton's dismissal rankled Hiram. The man was a total idiot. Even slapped with the fact his wife had left him, he refused to see the truth. "I'll call when I know something." He clicked off the phone, set it on his desk, and stared at it in disbelief.

His team lost Stevens before he left the airport. Annoyance bubbled up like lava about to blow. Hiram shoved his hand in his pocket and his fingers closed on the stone.

The answer didn't matter. Whether Nicole and Austin were working together or a third party had brought him in, finding him was imperative. Austin would lead them straight to the woman. Without a second thought, Hiram picked up the phone again and ordered the company's private jet. Obviously, he needed to handle the job himself.

*Port Santa Stefano, Italy*

The hostel was the fourth place Austin checked. As soon as he entered the lobby, he sensed Nicole would feel secure here. The lobby was clean, though the lumpy couches and the scared wood desk, tables, and chairs had seen better days. A place her husband would have dismissed. By far the safest place she could have chosen.

An older couple, mid-fifties, looked up from behind the battle-scarred desk that had barely survived the twentieth century intact. The scent of garlic and tomato paste permeated the lobby from beyond an open door he presumed was the couple's apartment.

The round faced man stood, eyes narrowed, recognizing Austin was not there for a room. "What can I do for you?" His assessment had Austin pegged as European. His question was in French.

Austin said nothing but slid a photo of Nicole across the desk. The man's pupils widened briefly, but then darted away. He pushed the photo toward Austin. "Not here. No one we know."

His wife shoved her way through the confined space to stand next to her husband. "Who is it? Let me see." She spoke in Italian.

Her husband snapped back, also in Italian, "Stay out of it."

A quick glance at the photo had the wife glaring at her husband. "I told you she'd be a problem." She turned away to storm toward their apartment.

"Wait," Austin said. "You may have saved her life."

The couple's faces reflected their surprise at his use of their native tongue but as his words took meaning the man's chest puffed, and the woman's brows drew down.

"Her husband is rich and powerful, but he was cruel to her."

"I knew it," the man said.

Austin was sure he hadn't known anything of the kind, but had helped the woman because she was beautiful and paid in cash. "Because you helped her, you've given her time to get away."

"She slept for two days," the woman protested. "We thought she was dead."

Austin nodded, hiding his shock. She'd wasted two days sleeping? She should have been using that time to get further away. Wait, holing up for a few days to regain her strength might have been the money move. If she was at flameout, pushing herself would have been foolish.

"When did she leave?"

"Yesterday afternoon with two other girls. Canadians. They asked about the bus schedule to Rome."

Austin slid five hundred dollar bills across the desk. "Others will come and ask about her. Say nothing. She's in great danger."

About to bolt out the door, eager to get to the helicopter and head to Rome, he stopped at the woman's deepening frown, tilted his head and waited for her to speak.

"They cut her hair and dyed it brown."

"Good." Maintaining a solemn expression was difficult when he wanted to shout with joy. Nicole was alive and likely in Rome. Her changed her appearance would make it harder for anyone to find her. "Do you have the other girls' names?"

The husband and wife exchanged another quick glance before the wife opened a drawer and took out a stack of photocopied passport pages. Within minutes Austin walked out of the hostel with what he hoped were the only copies of Kaitlyn Williams and Valerie Boyer's passport information.

# Chapter Eight

*Wednesday, January 18th*
*Rome, Italy*

Austin braced his back against the airport wall watching travelers negotiate the ticket windows with too much luggage. British Columbia was a popular destination. The all-night internet search had taken a toll on the hours he could have slept. There was a time that wouldn't have bothered him. Today, age and stress were definitely a factor.

He chose to stand to stay alert because he couldn't be sure when the girls would show for their early morning flight. Timing was everything.

For the first time in a year, his face was clean shaven. He felt naked despite his jeans and a new sweatshirt sporting a University of British Columbia logo. He glanced at his watch. Their flight took off in just over an hour. Where were they? Stiff from standing idle for the past two hours, he stretched.

The girls entered from the far door. The blonde, Kaitlyn struggled with a nylon duffle that was neither a backpack or had wheels.

Awkward luggage for traveling.

He kicked off from the wall and headed in their direction. Both women smiled, recognizing the UBC logo. He counted to five as he passed then he spun around. "Hey, I know you."

Both girls turned, each face expectant. Austin grinned his delight at running into old friends. "You're one of the Boyer's girls." Valerie's expression morphed into a dazzling smile. "You used to live in that big yellow Victorian on the corner."

Austin never failed to be amazed by what people posted on line. Valerie was delighted to be recognized and giggled as she held out her hand to shake his.

He snapped his fingers as though remembering something. "I think my younger brother took one of your sisters to the prom." It was a stab in the dark, but with three older sisters there was a chance he'd struck gold.

"You're Randy's older brother?"

She'd failed to release his hand and he smiled openly. Glad she'd chosen to flirt. Her voice had held a tone of doubt, so he added, "Step-brother, actually."

Amidst the girlish twitters and hand holding, Valerie asked. "Are you flying home?"

He had to remember this in the future. Airports were easier hook ups than bars.

Kaitlyn's open appraisal and hungry expression assured him a three-way wasn't out of the question. He stroked Valerie's hand with his thumb, pressed his lips tight, tilted his chin down, then frowned. "Actually just got here. Looking for a place to stay. Any recommendations?"

"We spent last night at a *pensione* near the train station. Cheap, clean, convenient."

"Sounds perfect." He laughed. "And we know they have a vacancy."

Both girls nodded. Austin hid his disappointment. Nicole hadn't kept the room. It was the smart move. She needed to keep moving, but it added another wrinkle to finding her.

Kaitlyn dug a card out of her pocket and handed it to him. Austin committed the address to memory. Maybe Nicole had her own room. He considered fishing for more information, but decided against it. "Thanks. I'll check it out. Good to see you again. I'll be sure and tell the Ran-man when I see him."

"Yeah, you too."

As he sauntered off he heard the blonde say. "I didn't remember Randy had a step-brother."

Nicole exited the side door of the

inexpensive *pensione,* pulled the charcoal gray hoody over her dark short hair and hoisted the backpack higher on her shoulders. She ducked her head and aimed her gaze toward the concrete walk directly in front of her. She clung to the shadows, working to make herself invisible. Clouds hung low in the gray sky. Along with the spiting rain the weather helped immeasurably.

Valerie and Kaitlyn had left for the airport hours earlier. Cell phones made one's life so much easier. Nicole hated abandoning hers on the ship.

She'd planned for months, made lists, checked details and still she hadn't prepared for everything. She should have purchased a cheap throw away phone to use. More than that – she should have gotten a fake ID.

In Rome, as elsewhere, payphones had vanished with changing technology. The train station several blocks away was her best potential source.

A door slammed. She jumped in alarm.
*Damn it, she shouldn't have reacted.*

After sleeping for two solid days, she could no longer sleep for more than an hour or two at a time. Her energy was drained, making each step a deliberate decision to continue moving.

Last night she'd tossed and turned. She

wanted to hibernate in the room, but in order to remain hidden she had to keep moving. But traveling without a passport was impossible. Damn her husband anyway. This morning when she was finally alone she'd combed through the miscellaneous items she'd dumped into her bag from the safe. The good news was his money belt contained almost ten thousand unexpected dollars as well as several credit cards she wouldn't be able to use. When she'd given Elena the hundred thousand dollars, she hadn't thought about how much money she'd need to survive. The bad news was no identification of any kind had her name on it. Linus must have tucked their passports in his jacket pocket when they headed off to dinner.

In the middle of the night a thought had come to her. Her only hope was the one man who'd offered to help. Austin Stevens. He had the rough hewn look of a man who would know how to obtain things that weren't necessarily legal.

Linus hadn't hired him which meant Austin might still be willing. Plus her husband swore he was gay. If he agreed to help it wouldn't be for sexual favors.

Sexual favors. She hated that term, but it was sexual favors that gotten her life so off track. Money, they said was the root of all evil. But money hadn't been the problem. The lack of it was what got her into this situation.

Nicole had no one to blame but herself if one didn't count her father, her sister and a car wreck that left Libby clinging to life.

Her sole goal had been to care for her niece, but medical care exceeded the salary of her measly assistant librarian position. In the end she chose her mother's path. She'd have to marry. And not just any man. Someone wealthy.

Nicole shook her head. With her history, she should have known a man would let her down. As a child she'd adored her father and he'd turned out to be a molester who publically ruined her life. Not just with his arrest and trial, but later on as well.

She choked back a harsh laugh and thought about how she, not Beth, had refused to believe it when the police came. Her father was innocent, but her mother piled them into the car in the middle of the night, grabbing only a few possessions, and had driven like a mad woman, careening around corners. Even as a twelve year old, she'd known her mother was driving too fast, but it was the scraping sound of the windshield wipers on dry glass that to this day made Nicole's teeth stand on edge.

Over her teenage years, her mother married and remarried. At eighteen, Nicole couldn't move out fast enough. As far as she could see, all a husband was good for was a broken heart and an empty bank account.

She hadn't loved Linus. Nor had he loved her. He required a certain type of wife. She needed a checkbook. Technically, they both got what they wanted, but the sub-plots got tangled.

After the ink was barely dry on the marriage certificate, his doctors insisted on institutionalizing Libby. Trapped, Nicole had no other choice but to agree. As Linus jetted between Lake Forest, Washington DC, his condo in Vail and his summer home on Lake Powell, he demanded his young bride be at his side. The first time she refused earned her a broken arm and a black and blue face.

Nicole understood her husband had orchestrated the doctor's findings. Whatever affection she'd felt for him soured. As a political spouse, she dressed the part, smiled the smile, and gazed adoringly, *à la* Nancy Reagan, but nothing more.

He retaliated with his fists.

Three months into their marriage she formed the beginning of her plan to leave. Two years, eight months and twenty-four days later, she'd jumped off a boat to save herself. If she got out of this alive, she'd never marry again. Hell, she never have sex either. Not that she'd miss that tedium.

She turned down a narrow path crowded with shops.

Two sneaker-clad feet partially covered by a pair of frayed blue jeans fell in beside her. "You are alone?" Asked a young accented male voice. "A *tourista*?"

He couldn't see her face. He knew nothing other than she was female and Canadian. Still he took a chance simply because she was female and alone. "Let me show you Rome. Is a beautiful city."

The man's voice held high drama and promise. Some might be fooled. She was not one of them.

Out of the corner of her eye, she saw his fingers reach for her hood. She scurried out of reach and darted into the first open doorway, pleased when the shoes didn't follow her inside the dark shop.

"Can I help you?"

Nicole raised her head at the sound of a female voice and let her hood drop to her shoulders. The voice belonged to a short, middle-aged Italian woman garbed in a thick black dress unrelieved by any adornment. Nicole opened her mouth to give her standard response indicating she was only window shopping when she took a serious look around the store. Artificial legs and arms covered the tables. Racks of bras stood in the corner. No wonder the boy remained behind.

"Are you in the right place?" the woman asked politely.

"No." Nicole smiled ruefully. "I was avoiding a man on the street. Would you mind if I stood here a few more minutes until he leaves?"

"He was bothering you?" The woman stepped forward. Her piercing brown eyes saw more than Nicole would have liked. "You are very beautiful. Men are always the same, are they not?"

Nicole sincerely hoped not, but she suspected the older woman was right. "Unless you have a male repellent, I don't need anything."

"But I do." Her eyes sparkled with delight. "Come with me."

She turned on the heels of orthopedic shoes and led the way to the back of the shop where hanging from the walls were canvas vests that housed a decided baby bump and larger, saggy breasts. This was exactly what she needed. Men would overlook a pregnant woman.

"My clothes are wrong."

The woman made a tutting noise as she lifted the heavy canvas over her shoulders and let it rest. "I can make you look like a proper Italian woman."

Not much later, even without clothes, the weight alone changed her stance. Nicole stared at herself in the mirror. She was transformed. A smile lit her face. The additional twenty pounds was offset by the weight lifted from her heart. Everything was going to work out. Linus would never find her.

She would be free.

# Chapter Nine

*Wednesday, January 18th*
*Rome, Italy*

Hiram Lynch's luxury private jet was met at Rome's International Airport by his six-member team. They scowled at the two harried local Customs officials as they attempted to enforce their rules. His men, used to being the top dogs, scoffed. Rules were for others.

Impatiently, they waited while Customs signed off on the flight and disappeared into the hanger. A low murmur of disgust punctuated by occasional curses accompanied the men as they entered the craft and made their way to the backroom, which doubled as Black Adder's office in the sky.

Hiram occupied the head of the plane's conference table and watched as his team, warriors out of place in a tame environment, filled the vacant seats.

Once he had considered himself a fighting man, but found the call of comfort appealed to him more than rooting around in the dirt, the mud and muck. He still kept fit, but wore his hair long so that corporate executives and government officials wouldn't mistake him for one of them either.

His plane reflected a lifestyle he couldn't have imagined fifteen years earlier, as did his home and swimming pool. Now he raised thoroughbreds and raced them. His liking for speed led him to investing in a NASCAR team. Life was good, because he'd learned one important secret. A person with money and vision could hire others to do the dirty work.

The ideal candidate for employment with Black Adder was a man who operated in the trenches. Hiram took in ex-military, giving preference to those from special ops, paid well, and demanded blood in return. Most gave it willingly. Whatever skills they possessed prior to being a part of Black Adder, his lieutenants honed into razor-sharp tools to be used worldwide.

Reichert sat to his left. He growled as he sat and his face wore a scowl. "Are we putting the Secret Service on hold while we hunt for a woman who most likely has drowned?"

Lynch narrowed his eyes and gave Reichert a disapproving glance.

Next to him, Mozart Jones asked, "Secret Service?"

*Oh, shit, he couldn't let this go.* Reichert should have known better than to blurt out information like that. "We're not here to discuss that. Let's talk about what we've found out."

He forced a smile, but Mozart had the tenacity of a bloodhound. Hiram would have to deal with this issue later.

Finding an assassin was easier than finding a man who could piece together an overall picture. For that reason alone, he'd come to Rome. Daily reports didn't relay the nuances of the situation. The men he chose followed orders.

Mozart Jones was a former SEAL and head of the diving team. Hiram turned to him first.

"We found her room underwater." He produced photos of the underwater room. "The patio doors were open and the safe empty. One of the life vests was missing from the closet. Leaping at the wrong moment could have trapped her under the ship. It's possible she drowned."

Lynch admired his thoroughness and studied the pictures. "But you don't think so?"

"No. I hacked into the ship's security cameras and viewed footage of the last minutes of the disaster before the electrical went completely out. Someone in the general location of her cabin wearing a life vest and a dry suit jumped overboard holding a bag."

Hiram's eyebrows shot up. Finally, a reasonable explanation for her disappearance.

"You think she might have seen this man escape and convinced him to get her to safety?"

"No. The jumper was between sixty-eight and seventy inches and slender. It matches the description of Nicole Layton."

Hiram laughed aloud and a couple of the other men followed suit. "Have you seen this woman? She's a princess." He tossed a photograph across the table. "Your theory would have taken months of preplanning. We know she couldn't sabotage the ship. And where could she have gone?"

Jones's deadly hazel eyes didn't blink. "It's one explanation."

Hiram scratched his chin and wondered if the truth could be this unbelievable. He turned to his team on the ground. "So, why is Stevens in town?"

"You were right. He was definitely interested in the wreck." Wildman Beastly pulled up a map of the region and spread it across the table. "Chartered a helo to the island." He stabbed the map with his stubby fingers. "We lost track of him after that, but he was somewhere in Rome as of last night."

Hiram glanced up from studying the map to look at his team. "You interviewed the pilot?"

Laser-Beam Ernst nodded. "Yeah, about an hour ago. Didn't get much out of him. Three stops. Giglio Island. Porto Santa Stefano. Rome."

"Where is Porto Santa Stefano?"

Beastly pointed toward a dot on the Italian shore.

Lynch waved to get the man to move his finger, so he could see the map. With his fingers he measured the distance between Giglio Island and the Porto Santa Stefano. Then searched for a legend to give his an idea of the distance. "What exactly did the pilot say?"

The Wildman shrugged. "Not much. Had some trouble understanding him. Claimed Stevens was an Italian, not American, and only used him for transport."

"Stevens's speaks fluent Italian," Jones said. "With his dark hair he might be mistaken for a native."

*That was an interesting bit of news.* Lynch studied Jones whose face told him nothing. "You know him?"

Jones's expression didn't change, nor did he seem overly concerned. "Former SEAL."

Lynch made a mental note to recheck Jones's history before turning his attention to the Wildman who continued his report. "The pilot waited at the craft for several hours until the other man reappeared at dusk, scowled and said, 'take me back to Rome.' The pilot's read was that the trip was a bust."

*Could that be true?* Hiram shook his head. "He found something. Otherwise he'd still be searching the coast. Let's divide up. Jones, you and Cartwright go to Porto Whatever and interview anybody you can find. Search the shore for any evidence. Even for a strong swimmer this would have been a distance. Reichert and Snyder stay at the airport. Watch planes bound state-side." He gestured at Ernst and Beastly seating furthest from him. "Hit the train station. Text as soon as you know something. I'm going to find a centrally located hotel and do a little internet research. We'll regroup tomorrow morning for a late breakfast."

Austin had missed Nicole by mere minutes. Maids cleaned the now empty room. Speaking the language had its benefits, but the cleaning staff knew nothing. Where would she go? Had she come with a backup plan? He wished he knew her better.

The *pensione* was located on a busy street, clustered with shops. He needed a different appearance. At the airport looking like a Canadian student was fine, but his face was too exposed. Inside the first retail shop, he purchased a knock-off Burberry raincoat, a plaid scarf, and a fedora. But even as the store keeper was ringing up his purchases, Austin's mind was elsewhere sorting details.

Nothing added up. She was terrified, running for her life, but had spent two days sleeping before partnering with random girls? Her planning had been superb, but what if she hadn't thought beyond getting off the boat? That would make her harder to track but easier for the wrong people to stumble across.

Sooner or later she had to get out of Rome, and he bet her plan was sooner. But where would she go?

The train station was only a few blocks away. He headed in that direction.

His cell rang. He considered not answering to prevent a distraction. But the few people he gifted with his personal number were those he'd promised to help. He stepped into an alcove and pulled the phone out of his pocket. Unknown registered in the screen.

"Hello." Silence followed. He stilled his impatient response of snapping out another 'hello' as he scanned the street. Where would she go?

"You said you would help me. Is that still true?" asked a soft female voice.

He froze. His outward focus shifted to his phone. Every ounce of his attention was now directed at the call and the voice on the other end. He couldn't be positive the voice was hers. Over the years he'd offered to help other women in similar positions, but his instincts told him this was the call he hoped would come.

"It is. What do you need?" He held his breath, needing to find the right words to get her to trust him.

"An ID." Her voice was barely above a whisper.

Good. She was getting to the point immediately. More than that it confirmed what he suspected. "Driver's license, social security card or passport?"

In the silence that followed he heard a PA announcement in the background. The words were muffled as her fingers covered the receiver to disguise her location. She was smart. She used a public payphone. The announcement and the location of the *pensione* made him hope she was at the train station. Immediately he walked in that direction. He wanted to run, but was afraid he couldn't control the change in his breathing.

"How much will each cost?"

Her caution about money worried him. Was she operating on a shoestring? Wouldn't it be just like Linus to keep her poor when he had millions?

"Let's worry about what you need. We can sort out the finances later."

The sound of an exhaled breath followed. "I need a passport and a driver's license immediately." Excitement edged her voice.

Relief rushed through him. He'd hooked her, but he still had to reel her in. "Good enough to get you on a plane? Or are you looking for a permanent ID?"

Judging by her silence, his question had stumped her. "You know who I am?"

He bluffed, "I don't offer to help everyone."

"Do you know where I am?" The underlying edge of fear coated her words.

He considered lying, but she was in too much trouble. He chose to shoot straight. "I have an idea."

Another announcement came over the background PA. This one in Italian and she didn't bother to cover the speaker. Yeah. He had a real good idea where she was. He picked up his pace covering the few blocks in record time. When he rounded the corner the main glass and steel entrance of the train station was in front of him.

He buttoned his new coat and wrapped the scarf higher around his neck. As at the airport, he saw no one to indicate the station was being watched, but that didn't mean the other team had left.

She hadn't hung up, but also hadn't spoken

in a few minutes. He tried to remember if he'd ever met a woman as comfortable with silence.

"Does my husband know?"

A long phone bank lined the wall. Almost every orange hooded area was taken. Austin faded into the crowd and positioned himself close to the corner. Was she safe or had she been spotted? He needed to get her out of there.

"I don't know, but others are searching for you." Even as he said the words he scanned the faces of the crowd. "There's an internet café near the Spanish steps next door is a camera shop. Email me a current photo and a name you want to use."

He expected more enthusiasm. When she didn't respond immediately, he added, "If you can get it to me in the next hour, I can probably have something for you tomorrow."

The whole thing was a lie. He only had a vague idea where the Spanish steps were located and had no clue if a cybercafé was next to it. All he wanted to know was had she been spotted. He continued to watch the long line of people and still couldn't identify her. Had she used another station? Was there another phone bank?

When he couldn't stand the silence for one more minute, she cleared her throat. "Okay."

The call went dead. No sign off. No nothing.

His breathing failed to return to normal.

Where was she? The entire time he'd been watching, people came and went but none of them looked like a thirty-three year old American woman. A frumpy, pregnant woman dressed in black pulled a scarf over her short brown hair and adjusted her backpack. He caught the flash of a Canadian flag.

An Italian woman with someone else's backpack.

Her posture sagged with the weight and the effort of moving with such a sizable belly. She glanced in his direction without seeing him. Teal. Gorgeous, stunning teal eyes.

Those eyes gave her away.

The pregnant woman was Nicole Layton. He came close to falling on his knees and thanking his lucky stars she'd appeared. A protective instinct swelled his heart, even as his brain denied what his eyes were registering.

He'd seen her just over a month ago. The pregnancy was either fake or enhanced, but either way he doubted the other agents would recognize her, particularly when she opened a pair of dark sunglasses that hid her eyes completely.

The Senator had been a fool. This woman was clever. Had her husband never looked beneath the surface of her beauty?

Despite her exhausted appearance, she

merged quickly into the crowd. He couldn't afford to lose her in the crowd and moved faster to fall in behind.

# Chapter Ten

Nicole swallowed the bile that threatened to overwhelm her as she trudged along the street, following signs to the Spanish steps. The one man she'd hoped could help wasn't surprised to know she was alive and in Rome. There was only one explanation.

Linus had hired him.

His response that he didn't know what her husband thought was a lie.

Taking the underground would have been faster, but she chose to walk. Panic swamped her mixing with jumbled thoughts. How had he been able to find her so easily? But she knew.

When the Senator needed something done, he hired only the best. In this case he was determined to find her, enough that he would even overlook his revulsion of the other man's sexual orientation.

She strode for several blocks, checking behind her to see if she was being followed. Twice she entered shops and stood at the window watching the street. Adrenaline pulsed through her veins as she steeled her backbone. Libby was safe. Even if they caught her, Nicole would escape again.

But how? The metro would take her to the edge of the city. Surely finding a place to camp for a night or two wouldn't be impossible, but she lacked a tent or a sleeping bag. Then what? Would she be back where she started?

Lack of sleep made her thinking fuzzy. She clamped her mouth closed when she realized she was panting. Not from exertion but from apprehension.

Where to go? No way could she go where he directed. That would be walking into the spider's web. No, she had to do this alone. She just couldn't think how to begin.

A hotel room required showing a passport. Camping wouldn't get her home, but it would delay her from her husband's grasp for another few days.

Cautiously, she looked over her shoulder for the hundredth time. Everybody appeared to be headed for a destination. Tourists with backpacks took pictures of everything in sight. Well-dressed Italian women with exquisite bags and high heels strode over cobblestones without tripping. Only she moved without purpose.

Her stomach growled. An outdoor café on the far side of the street beckoned. She crossed the street and found a table under the awning, partially hidden in the shade. Her tiredness overwhelmed her. She dropped the backpack and sank into the wrought iron chair with a heavy sigh.

All for nothing.

Linus knew she wasn't dead. Why hadn't she just let that little raft take her out to sea? Drowning would be preferable to going back to her husband. Too exhausted to think about food, she ordered a bottled sparkling water without lifting her head. Around her small island of loneliness was a sea of people speaking words she didn't understand, laughing and carrying on as if it was like any other day.

The chair next to hers scraped the concrete and the warmth of another human invaded her space as someone sat uninvited. A masculine scent, not cologne or aftershave, just male, drifted to her. For the silliest of moments a feeling of safety overcame her.

She raised her head and realized the joke. The masculine scent came from the seat next to hers. His fedora and scarf shielded his face. She reached for her sunglasses to get a better view.

"Don't take them off. Your eyes are too distinctive. I don't want people to remember you were here."

That voice. "Austin?" His name left her lips in a whisper. "How did you find me?"

"I followed you from the train station to

make sure you hadn't picked up a tail. Great outfit, by the way. The pregnancy thing totally surprised me."

His cheerful praise astonished her.

"Also, I liked how you moved on the street. Constantly checking to see if you were alone, ducking into stores and not following a precise pattern. That's clever stuff."

She frowned at him. "Not dazzling enough to lose you."

Momentarily she was distracted as he gazed in her direction. He'd shaved, giving his handsome, lean face a continental look. The electric blue eyes, shadowed by the brim of the hat, took in every detail. She shifted uncomfortably in her seat. Men had always stared, but Austin watched her with an intensity that made her think he could see her soul. She sniffed the air. He didn't smell like other men. No rich cologne, no cloying after shave, just male, warm and sensual.

What was wrong with her? He was about to sell her out, and she was acting like a girl with a teenage crush. Briefly she considered coming on to him, but she doubted she had the equipment to convince him to play for the other team. He'd probably laugh, and she didn't think she could take his rejection on top of everything else.

"I only found you because I believed in your

abilities." He scanned the street scene. "The men your husband hired won't be fooled forever. Plus they're suspicious I'm here."

The men her husband hired? Wasn't he part of that team? "Linus didn't hire you?"

He whipped his head around. "Is that what you think? That after I told you I'd help, I then offered myself to your enemy to hunt you down?"

"People will do anything for money. How did you know I was missing?"

"Layton called his insurance company to file his third claim for a deceased wife. You're insured for several million dollars, you know."

"I am?" She shook her head in disbelief. "I signed a bunch of papers when we married, but I didn't pay a lot of attention." Another thought occurred to her. "So you're not here to save me, you're here to tell the insurance company I'm still alive. How does that help me?"

He chuckled, a deep satisfied sound that lightened her heart stroked the back of his knuckle down her cheek. "Sweetheart, I'm not here to save you. You've already saved yourself. I'm here to help you get back to the states, and I have no intention of reporting anything about you to the insurance company."

Admiration filled his eyes. For the first time in days hope filled her soul, but getting back to the states hadn't been her goal. How candid could she be? Did she trust him? Was there a choice? "Could you help me get anywhere I wanted to go, even if it wasn't the states?"

He tilted his head as he studied her. "You stashed Libby in another country?"

It was all she could do to not react. This man appeared to know all her secrets. Was she sure he played it straight with her? Out of options she had no choice but to hope he told her the truth. Still she hesitated. He'd asked about Libby – calling her by name. He hadn't gotten that from Linus. Nicole doubted her husband even knew Libby's name.

"What continent?"

Well, that was vague. She could handle vague. "South America."

He stared at her thoughtfully. She refused to look away, but her skin tingled under his scrutiny. This was the kind of man she should have married. One who was honorable and took care of others. Too bad he was gay. Maybe it was true what other women said. 'All the good ones were taken'.

"What I really don't understand is, as smart and beautiful as you are, why didn't your husband do everything is his power to make you happy? You would have been such an asset to him."

Heat flooded Nicole's cheeks. She was ashamed, but he was the one person she wanted to understand the truth. "Linus believes he's the smartest man in the room. He wanted a certain look in a wife as an adoring arm decoration. I needed to protect Libby, so I never offered unwelcome opinions and he never sought them."

"You knew Libby needed to be institutionalized before you married him?"

"No." Her defiant tone registered in his eyes. "She needs medical help but not being locked up." Her lips twisted. "Linus' doctors insisted."

A wealth of understanding filled his expression. "You've been through a lot. I can see why you took the steps you did." From his coat pocket he took two passports. "I want to send a photo of your present look to my team at home. We'll need a nice hotel room where you can take a hot bath and have a massage to ease your muscles. I'll bet you're still stiff and sore from all that rowing."

She took the passport with stiff fingers that shook when she opened the pages to a photo of a blonde woman who vaguely resembled her. "Cathy Jones?"

He laughed low and deep. She stilled the tremor of excitement in her body. "And I'm Jim

Jones, your husband. Forgettable names."

"This picture isn't me. I'm not blonde anymore."

"We'll cover your hair with a scarf. When we check into the hotel I want you to clutch your stomach and sit in a chair with your head down until I come for you."

Her heart soared. He was going to get her out of here. Freedom was so close she could almost taste it.

As though he could read her mind, his eyes crinkled. "It's really going to happen." He dug in his backpack and removed two gold bands.

Nicole's wedding ring was tucked into her backpack along with all the other jewelry from the boat safe. Given a few minutes, she could have dug around and found the elaborate platinum band set with a multitude of diamonds. Like everything else her husband had given her, it had been chosen for someone else. For Linus, the words family heirloom meant sacred and allowed him to avoid shopping. Even the pearls in the Tiffany box had been part of the family collection and purchased for another Mrs. Layton.

Despite presenting it as a gift, any jewelry her husband bestowed was only on loan. The precious stones belonged to the family collection, not the replaceable wife. The original pre-nup she'd refused to sign stated something similar. There had been so many clauses she couldn't remember if that one had gotten eliminated.

The simple gold band Austin slipped on her finger meant nothing. Truly, it didn't.

But when he spoke the words, "M-m-marry me, Cathy Jones." She was pretty sure the slight stutter wasn't feigned. She wanted to throw her arms around him, kiss his chiseled lips until he gave up men and promised her happily ever after as Mrs. Jones.

She turned her head so he wouldn't see the tears that sprang to her eyes. Living in La-la land wouldn't get her home. As she gazed at her slender fingers with the simple gold band, she wished, not for the first time, that her father hadn't ruined so many lives, including her own."

# Chapter Eleven

He stuttered. He'd actually stuttered. Austin was stunned.

He'd put the ring on her finger and made a joke that fell flat because he stuttered.

Twenty-five years of his life vanished in the blink of any eye, and suddenly he was his father's son and a weakling.

Nicole Layton's take-your-breath away beauty gnawed at his soul. He wanted to erase the fear and worry in her sad eyes. Every cell in his body wanted to protect her. She needed him. This was what he did. He helped women.

But this was the first woman who made him wish he was another type of man – the kind who came home every night and dreamed of two-point-four kids, a dog and a country club membership. The kind who didn't wage war on the enemy and whose life-expectancy didn't shift daily. The kind who a woman like Nicole would naturally want, not as a white knight, but as a husband worthy of being her partner.

As soon as the words formed, he blanched, needing to erase the thought. He was nobody's ideal husband nor did he want to be.

Food arrived on large platters, crowding the small table. Saltimbocca, pasta, a tomato and anchovy salad with fresh basil and warm bread. The enticing smell of herbs and garlic danced on the air.

Nicole's stomach growled, and her cheeks pinked in embarrassment. "I didn't order this." She removed her sunglasses to gaze at the food.

He said nothing.

The day was overcast. No one was searching for a pregnant woman with a husband by her side.

"I did." He cleared his throat, pleased to have the stuttering under control. Speak slowly, calmly with deep breaths. "We need to eat. It's probably been a while since you've done more than eat on the run or pick at your food." He piled food on her plate and set it in front of her, then filled one for himself feeling more at ease being back in control. "Do you have a plan?"

Nicole pursed her lips and shook her head. "I was trying to decide what I needed to do."

"Well, I have a plan."

The hopeful look in her eyes made him smile.

"We need to lay low for a day or two." Her eyes were captivating like a cool lake on a hot summer day. He wanted to dive in, get lost in her.

*Focus on the job* he chastised himself. *Mooning around could get her killed.* He paused and gave a searching glance to the crowd to get his feelings under control.

"I chose a good hotel near the top of the S-Spanish steps."

*Nuts. There it was again.*

What was it about this woman that slipped under his defenses? Her beauty, even with her butchered hair and bad dye job, wasn't diminished. But it was more than her physical appearance. Outside, she was beautiful. Inside, she had what his SEAL team buddies called grit. Being in her presence jarred his senses, but even now, he held himself back not wanting to inch closer, despite feeling deep in his soul he needed whatever essence she gave off.

He cast a glance in her direction to see her staring curiously at him – not with pity or scorn that he'd seen in the eyes of others when he displayed weakness, but for the first time she was checking him out. She could have any man she wanted. There was something twisted here.

She ran her fingers through her short hair. "And… " she prompted.

Maybe he misread her. "I was going to say that I wanted us to look like a married couple on their honeymoon, here to see the sights, but too busy to leave the room."

He flashed his eyebrows. She laughed – a short, choppy surprised sound, making him want to pound his chest and howl at the moon in a caveman show of masculinity. What was wrong with him? Easing her frown shouldn't be that important to him.

He chose his words with care. "I think we've passed the honeymoon phase." He gave a significant glance at her belly. "But we can use the 'you're not feeling well' excuse for several days, if need be."

This time a small smile barely curled her lips. "All right."

He wanted to scratch his head. Most women he understood. She wasn't cool and distant, but she wasn't warm either. He fumbled to come up with a word that would describe her and settled on self-contained, but remained unsure if even that was correct.

"Eat while the food is hot," he said.

The fork filled with a dainty piece of veal lifted to her lips. She didn't bite. Instead she inhaled the rich aromas and closed her eyes to savor the flavors before the fork disappeared between her lips only to quickly reappear.

"Oh," she moaned. "So good."

Her pleasure in the meal caught him off-guard. He knew better than to stare at her lips and watch the fork slip in and out between them. His imagination didn't require much stimulus to fire on all cylinders. He forced himself to look away and dug into his meal. The food was good, but it didn't compare to the highlight of watching her enjoyment.

He searched for a safe topic of conversation. "Where'd you grow up?"

The startled look that crossed her face surprised him before her cool mask settled into place. "All over."

An answer that told him nothing, except that she had something to hide. He probed deeper. "Your father was military?"

"No." Her focus on winding the pasta on a fork was intense. "This meal is excellent. I didn't hear you order. Are you fluent in Italian?"

"Yes."

"I speak some school-girl Spanish, but I really don't have the ear for languages. It's a shame really."

Austin laughed as he tore a piece of bread from the loaf and dipped it in the sauce. "Is that how you did it? Every time you were asked a question, you deflected it back. No wonder your husband only saw what you wanted him to see."

She sat straighter in her chair. "Of course not, I thought we were having a pleasant conversation." Her tone turned cold. She speared her pasta with a sharp push of her fork. "How are we getting to the hotel?"

"By cab, of course I have a pregnant wife."

Their room had a charming balcony, a private bath and the largest bed she'd ever seen.

"I can sleep on the couch," he said before she asked, which made her realize she was staring.

The couch was short. He was tall. "Don't be silly. That bed would sleep Snow White and all seven dwarfs. I'm sure the two of us can share without impinging on the other's space."

Austin shed his outer garments with the easy grace of a man comfortable in his own skin. How she envied his casualness. She frowned when he turned and she could see the UBC logo on his sweatshirt. How young was he? Twenty-five? Twenty-six?

"So you think Snow White was kinky, too? Personally, I thought she had a thing for Dopey. You know, the short, silent type."

What? Why would he would say such a thing to her? Men didn't discuss sexual peccadilloes in her presence. She caught herself before she twisted her head to gauge her husband's reaction, but the familiar stab of fear had her heart skipping.

Austin didn't smile, but his icy blue eyes twinkled. "You're exhausted."

He unwrapped the long dark scarf from her

head and neck before tossing it to the chair. "Tomorrow, you'll think it was funny."

That was his idea of humor? A DC dinner she'd long forgotten flashed in her mind. Some comedian was the keynote speaker. Around them others had laughed, but Linus had seethed, chomping on the unlit cigar in his mouth. Nicole had sat frozen, afraid that any reaction would be paid for later.

Austin said she should have been an asset for Linus, but that wasn't true. She couldn't remember a time she hadn't been awkward and tongue-tied around others. If someone figured out who her father had been, she and Beth would be moved to another school.

High school had been a living hell. Boys had asked her out, but Nicole refused not wanting to experience an evening of agony trying to maintain small talk. By college she'd learned to handle herself somewhat better, but even innocent physical contact had made her jumpy.

The thing Linus had admired the most about her was that she was quiet. She spent three years making his opinions her own. No pantsuits. No loud colors. No questions. Still he'd erupted in anger. What she'd been to the Senator? Not an asset, but a huge disappointment.

A chill crossed her chest. Austin's fingers were on the buttons of her shirt. "What are you doing?" she demanded, struggling to cling to the material as he was easing it off her shoulders.

He raised an eyebrow, and she released the fabric, letting him remove the shirt. Her modesty wasn't in question. Under the black heavy blouse and skirt, she wore the pregnancy vest and another long shirt under that.

He laid the black garment on top of the scarf. "When we stopped at the store I purchased several things including shampoo, conditioner and soap – fragrance-free. Until we get you home… " He paused then corrected himself, "or where you want to be, I don't want any identifiable traces of odor on you. Right now I can smell your shampoo and your perfume."

He lifted her arm and sniffed her wrist. "And your lotion. Believe me, you smell great, but that won't work for us. The people hunting you aren't above bringing in dogs."

Nicole nodded her acceptance. She'd been surprised when Austin had pointed out a small store he wanted to enter. "Stand here." He pointed to a place near the window. "Watch to see if anyone looks familiar or is paying attention to this shop."

Several minutes later, lugging packages, he reappeared. "Are we okay?"

"I think so." He took her at her word and set off to locate their hotel.

Despite the fact he'd indicated they could take a cab, she'd preferred to walk. He wore her back pack and kept an arm around her as though helping her. They hadn't talked except for his occasional murmuring of instructions. At the hotel as he'd predicted the fake passport worked fine.

He lifted the pregnant bump from her shoulders and she sighed with gratitude for the reprieve.

"Heavier than I imagined," he said as he hung it in the closet. "I'm running a bath for you. Go ahead and take off the rest of your clothes." He tossed her a long white terrycloth robe and picked up one of the shopping bags to disappear into the bathroom.

He didn't shut the door, but she couldn't see him. The sound of water rushing out of the pipes had her hurrying to remove her clothes and don the robe before he returned. She didn't want him to see her naked. As Linus had frequently reminded her, her body would put any man off. Austin might be uninterested because he preferred men, but she didn't want to see revulsion or, worse, pity in his eyes.

"You ready?"

"Yes." Her voice emitted more confidence than she felt as she stepped into the bathroom, the large robe swamping her. Fortunately she was tall enough it didn't drag on the floor.

The oversized tub was filled with bubbles. Austin was arranging plastic bottles on the counter by the sink. "Get in. I'm going let you soak long enough to get the kinks out, but I'll come back."

She looked again at the tub and realized he'd blown up a plastic pillow for a headrest. Her brain was spinning. Why was he doing all this? "I showered this morning."

"I know." His grin caused her knees to clench as all her lady parts took notice of him. "But you need some pampering. And I need to doctor your hands. Getting out of here may turn tough and I want you remember this part of the journey had a few pleasurable moments."

He left the room allow for some privacy. She shucked the robe and slipped into the warm water. She sniffed. The warm bubbles had no scent. She closed her eyes. For a few minutes the world was being held at bay allowing her to stand down.

For that at least she was grateful.

# Chapter Twelve

Booting up his computer Austin waited for connections, then downloaded the photos he'd taken. He still couldn't believe he'd found her. The sooner he got her out of here, the better.

South America. Not what Austin would have chosen, but it was a good move. A smart move. She was a bright woman with a clever brain and a resourcefulness that awed him – all so carefully hidden behind a quiet demeanor and a pretty face.

Barely able to stop gazing he managed to email them to his brother. Walking back to the hotel, he'd wrapped an arm around her, tucking her in his side. His need to touch her was frightening. If he didn't get control, he was afraid she'd see him as one more man wanting to take advantage of her.

Using an untraceable satellite phone, he dialed Travis's number.

"Wow. I wouldn't have recognized her," was his brother's greeting. Good, he was online as well. "Except for those eyes."

Austin restrained his grin. He should have known his brother would have noticed exactly what he had.

"Colored contacts would have made her

impossible to spot. Good work."

"Lucky break." Austin didn't want to get into details. "We're holed up for the night. Have you figured out how her husband knows she's not dead?"

Even knowing the call couldn't be hacked both men were careful.

"One hundred thousand reasons. Is the child safe?" Travis asked.

"She thinks so and she'd been clever." In his mind's eye, Austin could see his brother nodding. "I'll get back to you as soon as I have the package. Stay cool." The package consisted of a passport that would fool Customs.

"You, too."

He disconnected the call. Up to now the op had been easy. The hard part would be to touch her bare skin and not indicate his interest. Hell, the woman made him feel like a puppy – a panting mongrel who wanted to lick her all over.

Enough. She was as skittish as a wild animal. One false move, and she'd bolt. Getting her into the states was going to be tough enough and would only happen if they worked as a team.

He had to face reality. She would never be his. Her only need of him was to get her out of here. Travis could get him a believable enough ID to get her on a plane, but not to survive long term. Customs wasn't a hotel desk clerk. They would look seriously at her photo, ask her questions and expect the two to match whatever story they devised.

There were still too many ways for her to be found.

He hadn't told her they were going to be joined at the hip for next couple of weeks while he worked out a way to get her husband off her trail. Linus Layton had infinite resources. Unless Austin was very, very good, it was only a question of time before he found her.

Austin pulled the sweat shirt over his head and tossed it on the dresser while he dug in his bag for a t-shirt. The bathroom door opened and the warm scent of the woman infused the room. He was so attuned to her he felt like a divining rod who had located a hidden underground well.

"I'm good to go now that I'm scent free." Her voice was soft and stroked his skin like fur.

He tugged the t-shirt over his chest. "I want you to practice an exercise I'm going to teach you. In periods of stress this will calm you. Inhale deeply for four counts. Exhale deeply for four counts. Do this in four minute intervals. Practice it now." Each time he said four he held up four fingers.

She sat on the bed and closed her eyes,

breathing deeply in and out. The exercise was effective. He could see the tension ease from her body and her face. After four minutes, he put a hand on her shoulder. "Slip off the robe and get under the sheet. I'm going to massage the soreness out of your muscles. We may have to move quickly in the coming days, and I want you at one-hundred percent."

"I can keep up."

"That I don't doubt. You've got hidden depths that most women are never forced to find. But we are a team and as a result we need to understand the other's weaknesses."

"So that means that after you give me a massage, I can give you one, too."

He grinned, hiding the terrified, yet thrilled lurch in his heart at the thought of her touching him. "Absolutely," he lied and turned away to give her privacy.

He heard the bed creak and the sheet shuffle as he drew the drapes and dimmed the light in the room. This would probably be the worse massage she ever got. No soft music, no incense, and no candlelight, but he had to know how her ribs were healing and if her bruises still showed like the ones on her arms. Could she go the distance or would he need to adapt his plan.

"It's not that I'm embarrassed. I know you're gay, but I feel weird because I'm so much older than you." Her voice was muffled by the pillow.

He snorted, wanting to kick his own ass. This was what good deeds got you. He skipped the gay comment for the time being. She'd probably be more at ease thinking that, but the age thing bothered him. "I'm two years older than you are."

The toned muscles in her back tightened as she harrumphed. "Only if you made a deal with the devil."

He closed his eyes as he warmed the oil in his hands, then caressed her shoulders, feeling the muscles give. "Of course I did. Years ago. I was eleven at the time." Slowly he worked his way up her neck, then down her firm arm.

She stiffened.

"Relax," he said. Instead she rolled to her side and tugged the stubborn sheet to cover her breasts. Slowly enough to allow him an intriguing glimpse.

He held firmly to her arm, continuing to massage each finger in her hand. "You're deceptively fit."

"We had a gym in the basement. I spent hours on the rowing machine once Linus announced the cruise." She tilted her head. Her teal eyes had darkened with the dim light of the room. "So what does an innocent boy of eleven get in return for selling his soul to the devil?"

He thought for a moment, before answering honestly. "Freedom from fear."

She studied his face, as though searching for answers. Her lips pressed into a firm line and she shook her head. "The devil is the embodiment of fear."

He shrugged, emulating a casualness he didn't feel. "Sometimes there are worst monsters out there." The room was very quiet. "You've obviously given this some thought. Have you never wanted anything so badly you'd give up your very soul?"

"Oh, yeah." Her voice was almost a whisper. "But how can you make a deal with the devil when he's your father."

Shock shook his spine. He'd thoroughly researched her. Why hadn't anything come up? "Your father?" He spoke carefully. "I thought he was a successful lawyer."

"That's my mother's second husband who adopted us. My real father ruined everything he touched including his daughters."

His hands stilled. *Oh, shit. Was it possible her life had been worse than his*?

The sadness in her voice tore at his heart. He really hated that he had to ask the obvious question. "He abused you?"

Slowly she shook her head. "No. Not me. Others. He liked little girls."

Too generic an answer. Her seething anger was personal. He lowered his voice. "Did he like your sister?"

She jerked her arm back, her eyes snapped, and her breasts rose and fell with her quickened breath. Within seconds she calmed and turned her, now cool eyes, toward him. "How did the devil free you?"

No longer content to sit, she rose to face him, the sheet covering her breasts. He reached for her hands, but she drew back.

Austin stood, paced to the window and back. Never had he told anyone his past. Not even his brother, but he needed her to understand that others had suffered at the hands of their parents as well. He returned to the bed. She scooted over a few inches, giving him more room. Instead of sitting, he lay beside her in the place she'd vacated. He folded his arms behind his head and was pleased when she lowered her body to lie next to him.

"My father was a heroin addict who would do anything for his next fix. My mother left him years before, but each time he'd find us. I made sure he would never find us again."

He starred at the darkened ceiling, fully expected to feel her move further away. Instead she laid her head on his shoulder and asked in a whisper, "You killed him?"

"Yes." He wasn't proud of his actions, but it had freed his family. He also wasn't ashamed. The normal timbre of his voice surprised even him. "And it was worth an eternity in hell. Since then I have killed many men in the service of my country, but he was the only man I murdered."

"I wish I'd had your courage." Her voice was so low he had to strain to hear. One of her hands rested on his chest and he covered it with his own.

"I was twelve when my father was arrested," she paused and took a deep breath. "For the statutory rape of a minor - several minors, actually. He spent eighteen years in prison. When he got out he begged my sister and myself to visit. I refused to go, but Beth went."

Austin closed his eyes and lowered his arm and wrapped it around her. Heartsick by her revelation. How she'd suffered. And yet to all the world she appeared like a Disney princess. The beautiful girl who married a rich Senator. With an ugly past to hide.

That explained a great many things. Layton couldn't have known. He wouldn't have risked his political career for her tarnished background. Unless he found out after he married her which might have explained his anger toward her. His research had confirmed Beth had been unmarried when she gave birth. Austin took a stab at the truth. "Why didn't your sister get an abortion?"

She was quiet for several beats of his heart. "Because when you grow up in a house like ours it is easy to lie to yourself. To believe everything will be okay if you just close your eyes. By the time she figured out that wouldn't work, it was too late."

He didn't want to ask, but he couldn't stop. "The car wreck that killed her. It wasn't an accident?" As he turned his head to study her face, he realized she'd long since shed all her tears for Beth and her child. Nothing was left but dealing with the cruel facts.

"I never thought so."

"But it fell to you to clean up the mess."

"Yes. Beth referred to her innocent baby daughter as an abomination. She wanted both of them to die."

He stroked her face with his thumb. He hoped he never met her father. It would be hard to avoid hurting him. "Was your sister as beautiful as you?"

She blushed. "Yes. Everybody will tell you how looks are such an advantage in life. All it ever brought the women in my family was trouble."

Austin knew to depth of his very bones that she wasn't out of it yet.

# Chapter Thirteen

*Thursday, January 19ᵗʰ*
*Rome, Italy*

Nicole nestled deeper into the covers. Even in hiding she couldn't lay around all day. But here she felt safe. Relaxed, even happy. Something she hadn't known for years. Certainly not during her marriage, when only a cold, dark emptiness resided in her soul. She stretched and could feel the residual pain in her ribs, but the tiredness had evaporated.

Talk about inappropriate timing. She rubbed her legs against the soft sheet. On the run, she wanted nothing more than to stop, let her heart sing and her twitching feet dance. For the first time since she was twelve, she had someone on her side.

Austin cleared his throat. She peeked over the coverlet. As he had the previous afternoon, he sat at the narrow table, hunched over his laptop. "Sleep well?"

"Uh-huh." She stretched. "You?"

He made an affirmative grunt.

"I don't know about you but I'm starving." She sat up in bed, pleased to see she wasn't naked. He'd dressed her in a t-shirt. One of his.

She sniffed the fabric, catching a whiff of his male scent. Her heart did a small jig.

As she scrambled out of bed, she twisted the fabric to make sure her naked butt was covered. The shirt hung to mid-thigh. Not that it mattered. Austin's strong hands had touched everything but the essentials during last night's massage. She'd fallen asleep somewhere in the middle and slept through the night.

Her toes curled into the soft carpet. Tomorrow she'd have a new passport and would be headed home. Well, not home, but as far away from Linus as she could get. She glanced at Austin whose attention was still glued to the screen. The daylight beckoned through the shuttered doors that opened onto the patio. She grabbed the handles and flung them wide.

Sunlight streamed inside. Goose bumps pricked her skin from the early winter chill but she didn't mind. The brisk weather affirmed her joy.

Below crowds swarmed the colorful shops. A mouthwatering blend of Mediterranean scents wafted upward from the cafes. Her empty stomach contracted.

A gust of cold wind wrapped around her body. Shivering, she closed the doors and opened the shutters to let in the sunshine. Heavy drapes covered the windows on either side of the doors, and she drew them back as well.

"Can we go out and eat?"

Austin glanced up from the computer and tipped his head as though weighing her request. "Sure. Get dressed. After you fell asleep last night I combined our luggage into a less distinct bag. Nothing other than your pregnancy should be memorable about us."

She pivoted around the room on her toes. "So I need to dress the part of your pregnant wife?" Dancing near his chair, she impulsively held out her hands in invitation. Judging by his grin her enthusiasm was catching.

He rose. "Every floor has cameras." He captured her around the waist and spun her in a circle.

Happy laughter bubbled up from within her and, without thinking, she pressed herself against him and brushed his lips with a light kiss. When was the last time she'd been this impulsive with anyone? Why she was now she had no idea, but it felt right. She looked into his eyes expecting to see him join her in laughter.

She was wrong.

Austin's arms tightened around her. The man who had become her buddy, her savior, and her friend was gone. In place of his friendly smile were smoky blue eyes that burned with flames of intent and lips that curled with a seductive promise.

How could she have believed he was gay?

Her heart pounded in her chest, and her blood turned sluggish. She hadn't wanted a man in years, but he was the one. The guy. The Mr. Jones she should have waited for.

For a few seconds everything hung unspoken in the air. Perhaps he waited long enough to allow her to protest although refusing wasn't in her vocabulary. Finally, with an exquisite, drawn out slowness, he leaned forward.

*Yes.*

Her body rejoiced. A shiver of pleasure ran down her back. She parted her lips, welcoming his touch. Unable to wait she pushed against him and took what she needed.

His body jolted, followed by a muffled laugh.

Just as quickly he tilted his head and mastered the kiss, neither an impulsive action nor a quick peck. No, he took kissing seriously.

Nicole had expected passion, yearned for it actually. But the longing took her by surprise. As soon as his warm lips touched hers, her willpower dissolved in a puddle. Nerve endings stirred, then tingled until her entire body was one huge erogenous zone.

One of his large hands swept under her t-shirt and up her back. She wanted to purr as his actions made her feel feminine and delicate. And possessed. A man hadn't indicated honest, caring, sexual interest in her in years.

She flung her arms around his neck and fisted her hands in his short hair. He was wonderfully tall. His erection pressed against her belly. She swerved her hips to stroke him as well. His hand cupped her buttocks and pressed her closer holding her in place. He lifted her off the ground and aligned her soft core to his length. His rough jeans abused her hot center in ways to delicious to contemplate. Her long legs wrapped around him. Her body arched into his and her nipples ached for his touch. She squirmed to get closer, rubbed her breasts against the soft t-shirt.

He lowered her to the bed, coming down on top of her. "You're killing me."

Her girlish giggle conveyed both her excitement and her nervousness. A shiver of anticipation left her trembling. He grasped one of her hands in his and brought it to his pants, folding her fingers over his penis. His huge, rock-hard penis, firmly encased in denim, strained to rip through the zipper. Blood pumped through his veins making him harder and thicker.

Reality hit her like a speeding train.

Sex had never been her friend. After the heady feelings evaporated, he'd want to control her. Nicole rested her head against his shoulder in a feeble attempt to harness her own body's response, refusing to let him see her panic.

"I've wanted you since that day in Illinois." The tone of his deep velvet voice reflected his desire. "If you don't feel the same, we need to stop now."

Just the sound of his rough, arousal-laden voice had her sex clenching. Moisture dampened her thighs. Not want him? More than anything in the world she wanted him. But a lifetime of experience screamed, *danger, danger, danger.*

If she said yes, would she open herself to another male domination? She'd never had a relationship that worked in her favor. Why did she think, when she was under the greatest duress of her life, suddenly everything would change?

Austin disengaged, taking the decision out of her hands, though her fingers still wrapped firmly around his penis hadn't let go.

"It's okay," he murmured. "I understand. Really, I do."

She released him, slid off the bed to the floor, knees tucked and head resting her head on them. How could she ever face him again? She'd been a fool. When would she ever learn?

He knelt in front of her, lifted her chin with a finger, and forced her gaze to meet his. No anger, only understanding. He dropped a peck on her nose. "Get dressed. Let's go eat."

# Chapter Fourteen

Where was his brain? Austin sat on the edge of the bed and willed his aroused body into quiescent. He had a job to do and taking advantage of the woman he helped would complicate matters – not even if she was willing. His body protested his loss.

Nicole was both smart and determined, qualities he admired. But she was a woman from an abused relationship who had a long way to heal before she entered into a relationship with a clear head and unblemished heart.

She would never be his and still, he couldn't stop the fantasy of her in his arms. One day she would choose another – a man who could offer her a lifestyle he couldn't.

Austin had helped a number of abused women start new lives. He and Travis had provided new IDs and safe places to live. Nicole might be gifted with those things, but she would never have the security of being invisible.

The new ID and hiding place would require she surrender her true identity. Hard for someone with control issues, but her distinctive beauty would be the thread that unraveled her safety. The money she'd taken from her husband would only keep her for a few months, maybe a year at best. Nicole would marry again. That man wouldn't keep her out of the limelight. Sooner or later Layton would find her.

The Senator was ambitious and her multi-million dollar insurance policy would go a long way toward launching a higher political office. She possessed enough information to keep him from his goal. The truth was Layton needed her dead.

Austin hung his head in his hands unsure what he could do to save her from that end. He shouldn't have agreed to breakfast outside and thanks to his blunder, remaining inside would be awkward.

He rose and checked the closets. The extra clothing wouldn't be missed if they had to make a run for it. The bathroom door opened. She emerged, dressed as the frumpy pregnant woman wearing little or no makeup. He donned his beret and tied a kerchief around his neck, then slung the new bag over his shoulders. Cautiously, he opened the door and checked the vacant hallway before gesturing for her to follow. "I don't know about you, but I need coffee. Are you warm enough?"

"I am. Shall we take the stairs?"

"Good idea." He took a deep breath and buried his apprehensions as they started down the stairs. Her steps were awkward as she lumbered down the narrow steps. "You really do look pregnant, you know."

Her shadowed eyes met his and while her lips smiled, he detected an element of sadness he hadn't seen before.

"Thanks." She pushed open the outside door.

The cool air and the warm sunshine were a perfect combination. Like tourists, they strolled, delighting in the sounds of carefree shoppers and fabulous architecture. Italian men lingered on every corner, making loud, rude noise to attract shoppers to buy puppets and umbrellas.

Nicole studied the shop windows. While she gazed longingly at leather shoes, Austin leaned against the wall and analyzed the surroundings and their safety. Nothing appeared out of place. Clusters of people chatted casually and laughed among themselves.

He relaxed, determined to enjoy what little time they could spend together. The nippy air put a pink tint in her cheeks, giving her youth and vigor even with her bad haircut and no makeup.

Her stomach growled, making him laugh. "Hungry?" A café with both sidewalk seating and a large interior loomed before them. "Let's eat inside."

He selected a booth near the kitchen over the

protests of the maitre d', but by doing so he had a clear view of the front door and Nicole was hidden by the high booth back. The popular restaurant was one large room with cozy booths lining the walls and larger family tables in the middle. If full, the room would be noisy and crowded, but mid-morning, they were between meals and the place was fairly deserted.

Austin kicked back, determined to look the part of the casual tourist.

The waiter appeared. "Cappuccino," Nicole said.

Austin held up two fingers and picked up the menu. "What looks good to you?"

The front door opened. He automatically glanced up. His body amped up to red alert. The faces didn't matter. He could recognize a warrior by stance and stride alone. The menu shielded the lowered portion of Austin's face. His beret covered his hair. He lowered his eyelids but kept watch behind his lashes. The seven men, walking single file looked past him.

Hiram Lynch led the team as he headed toward the largest table in the middle of the room. Austin almost swallowed his tongue when he recognized the well-known operative with his patented pirate hair bound at the nape with a leather tie. But it was the last man in line who panicked him. Austin slid as far toward the wall as the bench seat would allow, shielding him from their direct vision.

His SEAL swim buddy – a guy who knew him inside and out – Amadeus "Mozart" Jones.

Well, now he knew how the divers had slipped into the water and searched the ship without permission. Mozart was one of the best. What Austin couldn't figure out was how the Italian authorities found out they'd been there at all. His swim buddy had never been careless.

What was the head of Black Adder doing in Rome? Two of his men were the ones Austin had seen at the airport. This was who was after Nicole? The stakes spiked significantly. The answer narrowed to one simple fact: the Senator had no intention of his wife being found alive.

"What?" Nicole whispered.

He held a finger to his lips.

She'd mimicked his movement of sliding across the seat. "Can you come to this side?"

He shook his head. The waiter arrived with their coffee drinks.

"Order for us." He dialed Travis's number. The time change of nine hours meant it was after one in the morning in Portland. Travis answered on the first ring.

"Hang on." As Nicole ordered, Austin turned his head to not be overheard. "We've got a problem."

Travis waited while Austin outlined the situation using as few words as possible.

"Mozart and Lynch? You're sure?"

Austin could hear his brother's mind working. "Positive."

"What time is it in Rome?"

"Ten-twelve."

"I'll call you back in a few minutes."

Nicole's gaze flitted around the room. Her lips were drawn in a tight line and the bottom one had been sucked entirely into her mouth. She reached for the coffee with trembling hands and leaned across the table. "I'm so sorry I suggested we go out. What are we going to do?"

Reaching for her hand, he nodded to reassure her. "Eat breakfast. Travis will figure out a plan." He attempted a calm pat of reassurance, but even that brush with her skin sent electricity up his arm.

She jumped at the contact, but then clutched his hand in both of hers. "You're sure?"

Austin smiled with confidence and squeezed her hands before he released her. "It's what he does best."

As soon as this op was over, he needed to contact Mozart, because the one thing he absolutely believed, the former SEAL wasn't cut out to be a mercenary. He only hoped the other man wasn't in too deep. He pushed his cell phone to the edge of the table and surreptitiously took a few photos. A seven-man *team* was overkill for this job.

The insurance company had given the brothers a few days lead-time. That time would save her life. If she hadn't called yesterday, she would have been in deep trouble before he could have gotten to her.

She huddled in the corner. His chest constricted. If he could get her to safety, he wouldn't be able to let her go. To hell with men who could afford her he wanted her and she needed him. And he vowed to do everything in his power to win her.

The food arrived and she shoved her plate of eggs and toast further away.

"Eat," he said. "We may not be able to stop again." He moved her plate in front of her and waited until she picked up a fork. "All of it."

He leaned over to check out Lynch's table. A man he didn't recognize spoke and gestured at a map. The rest of the men listened intently. No one smiled or joked. Every man wore an expression that looked as if he'd come from his mother's funeral.

Austin sat back and picked up a fork as he considered what that meant. He'd barely eaten two bites when his phone beeped. Travis. He handed one earpiece to Nicole and took the other.

"I have a plan," Travis said.

Austin gestured toward Nicole to have her lean in. "Go ahead, we're both on the call." Nicole's brow knit in a frown. He should have told her Travis was a master strategist.

"If Nicole was alone would they recognize her?"

"Not if she wore sunglasses."

"Good. Have her leave, take a train to the airport and wait for you there. You two, are going to hitch a ride on Lynch's company jet. I'm sending a schematic of the interior and the hanger location."

"How do we know when he's going to leave?"

"That's part two of the plan. Disinformation. Once Nicole's been out of there for ten to fifteen minutes, stroll over and surprise them. Make it look like you've been following them."

Austin couldn't help himself, a deep chuckle tumbled out. Leave it to his brother to pull the audacity card.

"Here's your play: she's been found dead. I'm setting up an Italian news feed that will indicate her body was trapped in another part of the ship. Show them your phone or let them discover it themselves. Wish them luck if they want to stay but you're going home."

A million objections sprung to Austin's lips, but he caught Nicole's nod. She could see how it would play out. Hell, she and Travis agreed. Who was he to argue? But a little note of self-doubt crept in. "What if they don't believe me?"

"Well, they're not going to shoot you." That wasn't as reassuring as Austin would have preferred. "If they follow you, lose them. Or take them with you to the airport, then shake them.

In the meantime, the FBI deputy director is calling Lynch and demanding he show up in his office in the morning on some trumped up charges."

In the twelve minutes Travis had been off the phone he'd been busy.

"You got Aaron Cleves to do that?" Austin asked.

"He owes us. They would have never pinpointed Taggart without our help. He was glad to do it even though I woke him up. He's calling in exactly one hour so get your act together before then."

"We're in motion now. We've got everything with us but a few changes of clothes which we can abandon. She can leave from here for the airport."

"Nicole, you'll look out of place at the hangar, so meet Austin at the terminal. Choose an out-of-the-way destination in case the others follow."

She pulled sunglasses out of her pocket, slid them on and was ready to slide out of the booth. "Where?"

"Any public place you feel safe. I'll find you."

At her raised eyebrow Austin suppressed a brief flash of guilt that he'd tagged her baby bump with a GPS tracker along with the one in her purse.

"One more thing," Travis said. "Watch your back. Lynch and his henchmen may not be the only group on the hunt."

Nicole hesitated before asking, "What if they follow me?"

"Austin tells me you're clever and have instinctive street smarts. Find a way to ditch them." Travis cleared his throat. "Have you got anything she could use, like a taser?"

Austin thought about the small selection of weapons he had in his bag. The best he could do would be a knife or a gun. Nicole was fit, but anyone with training would be able to disarm her. "She'll do better with her wits than a weapon. She's smart."

Nicole's lips curled in a smile. Either his comment pleased her or she was relieved not to have a weapon.

"You're right. Plus they'll want to take her

alive, not kill her."

Austin said nothing, not wanting to alert her to his suspicions. Travis was wrong on that front. Nothing about the men at that table screamed rescue party. What the hell had Mozart gotten himself into? And why?

# Chapter Fifteen

Austin was still chuckling as he searched for Nicole at the airport. Travis had called it right. Austin had added his own special twist, of course. He'd crawled out a bathroom window and come around to the front of the building, losing the beret and kerchief and adding à sports coat.

The change was enough the maitre d' offered to seat him again.

Austin spotted Nicole sitting at the back of the airport sports bar. Her face lit up and her body sagged in relief when she saw him. An empty pint glass rested on her table.

He raised an eyebrow in amusement which she ignored. Her head bobbed and weaved as she scanned the surrounding crowd. "How'd it go?"

He grinned, dropped into the chair next to hers, and flung his arm around her shoulders. "Keep it subtle," he cautioned as he clasped her chin and turned her face toward his. "It was smooth. Exactly as Travis predicted. You should have seen their faces when I plopped down at their table. Three of them drew guns. What idiots. Made a woman, two tables over, to scream. Lynch scrambled to chill her out. Did you eat?"

Her eyes were the size of saucers. "No. How did they react to the information?"

"Disappointed, mostly." He refused to tell her that Lynch could have charged more money, if she'd been found alive and then been quietly dispatched. Nor did he add that Mozart gave no indication they'd known each other. Curiously though, Lynch's eagle eyes had tracked the interaction between the men.

Nicole knit her brows. "What now? I got us some snacks and bottled water for later."

"Good idea. You ready?" At her nod, he helped her rise, dutifully assisting his pregnant wife. What would a child of theirs be like? Tall for sure. Loved. He shoved his errant thoughts aside as he steered her toward the side exit. "I was going to suggest we walk, but let's grab a cab for speed. We're ahead of Lynch, but not by much."

They found the hangar without problem. Austin smiled, let out a breath. The hangar doors were open so he wouldn't have to jimmy the lock. But open doors meant people were around. He needed to get into the plane without being seen. He held a finger to his lips.

She tugged on his sleeve. "How are we going to get inside?"

He frowned. "Walk in?"

Her response was to punch his arm. "Not the building. The plane."

"It's not locked."

"Really? How do you know?"

"Private jets are kept in secured hangars; no keys are required to get inside."

She was silent for a minute or two before asking, "Can you fly a jet?"

He nodded. "Pretty much I can fly anything designed for air travel."

He didn't see anyone around, nor could he find any security cameras. He raised his finger to his lips for silence and pulled her toward the plane. For a woman he regarded as one of the quietest women he'd ever met, now that he needed silence, she had questions that couldn't wait.

"Can we steal the plane?"

He choked. They had created a monster. "No. This isn't Grand Theft Jet. Besides I'm not crazy about orange jumpsuits."

Quickly, he opened the plane door and lowered it, catching it before the chains clanged as they were pulled tight.

He put a hand to the small of her back to urge her up the stairs. "Hurry."

Nicole ran up the short ladder, her baby bump slowing her down. Once she was inside, he stepped in behind her and tugged the door shut.

She waited in silence until he turned. "It's hot in here."

"I know. Until one of crew shows up we'll have to live with it. According to the schematic, closets are in the back room. Strip out of that baby bump otherwise it will be hours of misery."

"We won't need disguises?" Her tone told him she thought the baby bump made her invisible.

"With a tail wind, the flight should be about nine hours to DC. You'll be more comfortable without the extra weight."

Worry had her gnawing at her bottom lip. "What if he finds us?"

Austin took her face in his hands. "I'll take care of you." Driven by impulses that surprised him he lightly kissed her lips. "You'll be safe with me. Lynch probably has security clearance that means he'll bypass customs. Depending on where he parks, we could be on another flight to Portland a couple of hours after that."

The muscles in her face relaxed and he reluctantly let her go. He desperately wanted to keep her in his sight, but busied himself looking around while she changed clothes.

The jet gleamed like nothing he'd ever seen. The front room simulated a comfortable living room with reclining buff-colored leather chairs. A light, highly polished wood was used throughout including the doors to the cockpit and bathroom. The tiny kitchen had a fully-stocked bar near the cockpit. The rear of the plane had an open floor plan with a conference table that sat ten. A second bathroom and two closets were in the very rear of the plane. One closet hid a large copier and a second had several empty hangers and two sports jackets. Bench seating under the windows held storage underneath.

The biggest problem was the long corridor which ran the entire side of the plane. If they were noisy, someone sitting in the front might hear. The closet doors were movable louvered slats probably designed to keep the copier cool.

Austin found a stack of blankets and pillows in one of the bins. "We're traveling in style, but our seating is in steerage." He studied the layout again. "Once the flight's taken off, I think we'll be safe. We can stretch out on the closet floor."

Nicole had pulled off her shirt and the baby bump which she placed on a hanger. Working in her utilitarian white bra and elastic bandage, she knelt on the floor and spread out the numerous blankets to create softer padding and plumped up the pillows she'd positioned at the top. Her face glistened with sweat. As she rose, the tops of her breasts jiggled. He couldn't tear his gaze from their velvety softness.

The nest she'd created meant they'd be stretched out in the dark side-by-side for hours. Austin hadn't considered the intimacy of it. He restrained the groan that leapt to his lips.

Nicole dug in their bag until she found a pair of lightweight pants and a white t-shirt. She tossed the shirt over her head and glanced over her shoulder in his direction. "Are you wearing that?"

Apparently, not.

"Uh, no." He fumbled sounding like a school kid. A woman in her underwear shouldn't affect him like he was fifteen.

How much was he willing to take off? His jacket and hat, sure, but he also removed his belt and slacks and hung them up as well, donning a t-shirt and a raggedy pair of jean shorts. She'd dressed in a pair of Capri pants in a shade of blue that almost matched her eyes and hung the heavy wool shirt in the closet beside his clothes. She looked smart. Even the oddly cut and colored hair looked good with the change of clothes.

"You have a tattoo." She gestured toward his armband tribal tattoo that peeked under the sleeve of his t-shirt.

He shrugged. "More than one. I got them

when I was young. Now I wish I hadn't. Real frankly, I wouldn't let a child of mine get one."

Her fingers froze in the air. "You have children?"

"Uh, no." He paused, then added, "Not yet."

"But you want them?"

The question caught him off guard. Did he want children? For years he'd said no children, no wife and definitely no marriage. That wasn't the life he planned for himself. What kind of parenting skills could he have? But suddenly he wasn't so sure. Certainly, children would change his life. As would a wife, not just any wife, but a woman he truly loved. Would he agree to children?

Nicole moved efficiently about the cabin. For a woman like her, he'd agree to anything just for the pleasure of seeing her smile. Instead of answering her question, he asked, "What are you doing?"

She removed a smaller zippered bag. "What does Lynch drink?"

Austin shook his head. "Don't know. Why?"

"The biggest feature in the other room is a bar. I'm betting drinking is a big part of his life."

"Probably," Austin agreed. He followed her to the front of the plane after tugging on shorts.

The bar was fully stocked and no bottle appeared more important than any other, but

Nicole dropped to her knees and unlatched the storage area underneath. "There are six bottles of Wild Turkey and only one or two of everything else."

"Okaay," he said, drawing the word out, still unsure of her plans.

Nicole popped up and grabbed the open bottle of Wild Turkey from the front of the bar. She held it up to the light. About three inches of golden liquid remained in the bottle. She unscrewed the top and produced a small tube he hadn't noticed in her hand.

His heart zipped into his throat. Was she going to poison Lynch? He touched her shoulder. "What's in there?"

"Ground up sleeping pills."

Her answer relaxed him somewhat. "You carry that with you?"

"Mmm-hmm. It's turned out to be surprisingly helpful. What are you doing?"

"Adding a couple of cameras."

"Can I help?"

"Turn on my tablet. Let's see if we've got a clear picture."

Before Nicole got the computer out of the bag, Austin heard voices outside the plane. He inched to the window and peered out. A small group of men were standing beside the wing. Two guys looked like mechanics, but the other two didn't.

The pilots had arrived. Lynch wouldn't be far behind.

# Chapter Sixteen

The closed-off interior of the large private jet was warm, but the closet, which when empty had looked big enough to hold two adults, was stifling hot. Nicole was crushed, lying between the un-giving wall and Austin's overheated body – a dilemma, both delicious and unbearable. He cracked the louvers and a cooler stream of warm air seeped through the slits. She inhaled desperate to draw air into her lungs.

"You okay?" he whispered, turning his head so that he could look at her over one shoulder. Sitting was awkward, reclining was worse.

"Yes." She adjusted her position to see through the slats to no avail. The slits barely cracked could be seen through, only if one was next to the door and looking upward. Getting closer to Austin was a temptation best avoided.

His arms were amazing. Biceps that he didn't need to flex were massive. His muscles were so tightly banded together thick veins stood out on his skin. Long powerful fingers made his hands the sexiest she ever seen. And that tattoo. Not a great fan of inked arms but his spiked armband made her weak in the knees.

"Who's here?" Even whispering in his ear

was intimate.

His scent overwhelmed her. He was fearless. They operated with a sketchy plan at best. His confidence propelled them forward. Alone she would still be wandering around Rome hiding. The men Linus had hired would have eventually succeeded. After seeing them in the restaurant, she had no doubt. Seven. How could they not find her? How much had Linus paid to have her found? As she'd slunk past their table her legs had wobbled. To an onlooker she'd been upright, but her inner personality had been curled into the same ball as the Senator's wife.

Every day without Linus was a blessing. A few wonderful moments of freedom. If caught, her fate would be worse than drifting out to sea on that little rubber boat.

And she had Austin to thank for finding her. She sucked in air, wanting to breathe in his bravery as well.

"Two pilots." He turned his head to speak and his warm breath tickled her ear. She was practically sprawled on top of him, but he didn't move away. "Can you see?"

"No."

He sat upright, batting his hand at the clothing that hung above their heads. Even though Nicole had squeezed the hangers together, head room was at a premium.

The glow from his tablet lit up the closet. "Scoot over." He lifted his body and indicated she was to shift next to the door.

Lying flat she could view most of the room through the slits. He stretched out. The length of his body touching hers as he held the screen for them to watch. The cameras he'd installed showed angles of the front room. Both were vacant.

"Where are they?"

"Cockpit, but if one heads this way, we'll know."

She rolled to her side to give him more room. Propped on her elbow his face was shrouded in the light from the tablet.

"You can use my shoulder for a pillow, if you want." He opened his arm to welcome her closer.

Should she? She froze. A thousand reasons to refuse ran through her mind, but her body nestled tighter to him until she was practically lying on top. With one arm tucked next to her, she laid the other across his chest and gradually sank into the toasty welcoming comfort he offered.

The engine roared to life, and Nicole felt a slight rumble in the floor Austin cracked the door which allowed cool air to enter.

"Will we be safe?" She had no idea why she

asked the inane question, but for some reason she needed to hear Austin's voice.

He stroked her bare arm. "Are you a nervous flyer?"

"Only when I'm a stowaway."

He laughed quietly, bursting the bubble of anxiety rising in her chest. "Remember those breathing exercises. Do them with me."

Together they breathed as one. Nicole's tension eased, but Austin who was always calm, became Zen-like. They lay in comfortable silence for a while.

"What do you usually do during a flight?" he asked.

"I read or watch a movie."

"I've got books and movies on here." He indicated the tablet with a nod of his head. "If Lynch sleeps, we might try that."

While his tone gave nothing away, Nicole knew he offered to entertain her against his better judgment. This was a man trained to be on the alert. His job in which she suspected he excelled, was to save her sorry ass and get her to safety. Not because anyone was paying him, but that was the kind of man he was – a man who righted wrongs – a man who came to a woman's defense.

At the same time he gave her things he shouldn't – like breakfast at the café and letting her use the tablet for foolishness. His problem was niceness. If he hated to refuse her, she vowed to be stronger and not ask for things she didn't need.

The back of a pony-tailed head popped into the screen. "Lynch is here." Quietly Austin slid the door closed and tightened the louvers.

Lynch tossed his luggage, a black duffle, onto one of the seats and disappeared to the left. Several minutes later he emerged, a scowl on his face, followed by one of the pilots. The pilot walked straight toward the camera. Nicole held her breath. He was close enough she could see the scar that separated one eyebrow and the slight dimple in his chin.

Austin stroked her arm with more vigor, and Nicole uncurled her fingers, digging into his chest. "Sorry."

The pilot bypassed the camera. Austin opened the door a fraction and turned his head. "He's closing the door. We're in luck. There's only Lynch and the two pilots on board."

On the screen Lynch plopped into a chair, directly in view of the camera. How had Austin known exactly where the man would sit? Lynch pulled out a laptop and kicked the recliner back.

The pilots didn't linger. Within a few minutes, the wheels under them were rolling. The jet taxied for several minutes. She closed her eyes and listened to the beating of Austin's heart while the gentle stroking of his hand warmed her soul. The plane picked up speed. Nicole stiffened for take-off.

"Relax. We're going to be here for awhile."

She opened her eyes to see that the tablet was wedged against the wall off to the side. Without thinking about it she raised her leg and curled it across his thighs. He grasped behind her knee and tugged it higher. What would it be like to lay next to this man forever? To be part of his life? She inhaled his scent. She knew the feeling of safety wouldn't last but she desperately wanted to enjoy it while she could.

They stayed together not moving for what seemed like hours, but in reality was less than forty-five minutes according to the clock on the face of the computer. The plane reached cruising altitude and leveled off.

Austin opened the closet door. Nicole was rejuvenated by cool air. "Stay here. I'll be back." He untangled his body from hers. The loss left her bereft.

Shaking off the unfamiliar feeling, she clambered to a sitting position as he crawled into the room. Even on his hands and knees, he exhibited grace, rising to his feet after he'd cleared the doorway. Needing something to do besides fret, Nicole smoothed the blankets that covered the floor.

Across the room, Austin peaked around the edge of the room's partial wall. She pushed the on-button for the tablet to see what was happening in the front room. Lynch slept in the chair, his laptop still open with an empty glass beside it.

Austin crossed in front of the camera and tossed her a quick grin. The one thing she had learned about the Stephens brothers – they didn't lack for moxie. Austin lifted Lynch's laptop and moved out of her line of vision. She waited. Several minutes later, he replaced the laptop angling it exactly as before.

He squatted down beside the conference table. "Lynch is asleep, snoring hard. The Wild Turkey's almost empty. We can relax a little."

She scooted out of the closet but stayed by the door. If they had to move quickly she wanted to be ready. The tablet she propped against the door so both could see the screen.

His eyes crinkled. "It's frightening how smart you are."

His approval lightened her heart. She stretched her legs, pleased by the compliment. All her life she'd been pretty, she couldn't remember someone admiring her for her brain. Her sister, Beth had once declared if Nicole lost her looks, she'd have nothing. Apparently

Austin didn't agree.

"I can put on a movie if you want."

She leveled a doubtful look his way. "Do you have any girl movies? If my choice is between sports or fighting shows, I'll have to pass."

He laughed quietly. "I might surprise you.

Once again his confidence showed. She really knew very little about him. "Tell me about you."

His eyebrow quirked. "This sounds suspiciously like, 'Tell me about the rabbits, George.'"

She gasped, choking back a startled laugh. A man who quoted Steinbeck? "You surprise me. I thought you'd go for something along the lines of…" She thought for a minute. "Tell me of your home world, Usul." Delighted she'd come up with a guy's movie he would have seen.

He grinned. "Never would have pegged you for a Dune fan."

"You're stalling."

"Not much to tell. I have two brothers. You've met Travis. Sam, or The Cube, as we used to call him is a police detective in Portland."

"The Cube?"

"Long story."

Like they were going someplace? "We've got

time."

Austin adjusted his position, getting more comfortable. His eyes were relaxed, happy. It was the first time she'd seen him truly at ease.

"Sam's real name is James Eugene Sampson, Jr. His father died when he was young and his mother remarried a real asshole who called him Junior with as much malice as he could master. In defiance James became Sam when he shortened his last name. Then to piss his stepfather off even further, he figured out that Sam Sampson was S-S-S. All through high school, he was S-cubed. By the time he became a SEAL, it was shortened to The Cube."

She smiled. Austin may have had a terrible childhood, but he had brothers he loved. "He sounds like the cocky one. Why is his last name different from yours?"

Austin stared out the window. Nicole turned her head to see what he saw. Nothing, but sky. His face had lost its glow.

"He was cocky, confident, swagger and all. The cool kid in school. Played football. Wanted to go pro. When his stepfather lost his job, he took up drinking. One night he tried to kill Sam with the metal pipe and almost succeeded. I brought him home. My stepfather, Rod, was a good guy. He never said anything, just co-opted Sam into the family with the rest of the kids."

A quiet smile curled his lips. "Rod believed being a SEAL was the most honorable profession in the world. While he didn't have any sons of his own, he convinced all of us to go into the Navy."

Nicole was surprised. Not that Austin had been a SEAL, she'd figured as much. "So all three became SEALs?"

"Yep."

"Isn't that against the rules?"

He nodded, his eyes crinkled. "Travis joined first. Then Sam – not a blood brother and somehow the Navy missed the part that he lived in the same household, but they refused to let me apply because the Navy doesn't allow brothers to be put in harm's way."

"What happened?"

He chuckled. "Skid Rowe happened."

"Is that his real name?"

"No, his real name was Michael. He was from some backwater community in the Ozarks, had sandy red hair and freckles and this open, friendly face. But smart. Oh, man, he was smart. He loved explosives and was good with them. Kept the whole team calm, telling jokes, yuking it up like a big, happy puppy. He pestered the Navy, writing letters, hounding the brass until they reluctantly let me try out for the SEALs. I'm sure they were hoping I would ring out."

He glanced in her direction, then clarified before she asked. "Quit. But I didn't. With two brother already SEALs there was no way I could give up. Unlike many of the others, I knew what to expect."

While he told the story in an amused voice, his mouth tightened into a firm line and he stared at the ceiling.

"So what happened?" she asked in quiet voice, trying to decide if she wanted to hear the ending or not.

"Iraq happened."

She hung her head. This was going to be worse than she'd imagined. She waited, remembering her yoga and the deep cleansing breaths as she strove for serene.

"There weren't enough bomb-sniffing dogs. The one we'd been using had gone with another unit. Our team crested a hill. A Zodiac waited at the bottom to take us out of there. I can remember my boots hitting the ground. We were running." He shook his head. "Then we weren't."

Nicole closed her eyes and visualized the scene as Austin's soft, sad voice washed over her.

"A bomb exploded around us. I was thrown against the wall of a house. By the time I picked myself up off the ground, every muscle ached and my head was ringing. Warm water trickled down my neck, but when I raised my fingers to wipe the moisture away, they came back bloody because my ears were bleeding."

Nicole opened her eyes to see his gaze lost in memories.

"There were six of us. The Cube, Skid, Demon, Jake-the-Snake, Mozart and me. My legs were shaky, but I used the wall for leverage and forced myself to a standing position. Dirt and rocks rained down from the sky. I couldn't hear. My eyes told my brain we were in the midst of chaos, but my mind refused to believe it. My stomach turned over. I'm puking my guts out, which I could smell and taste, but couldn't hear it. It was a dream gone wrong."

Austin rose from his position and now paced back and forth as he relived the horror of Iraq. "The dust settled. That's when I saw the crumpled body in the middle of the road positioned wrong. I crawled across the road, coughing, choking on the dust and debris. The sharp sting of pebbles, glass, and concrete on my palms and knees broke through my numbness."

"Jake-the-Snake Jackson, the team medic, lay in the middle of the road, half his face blown off. A featureless, grizzly red and gray mass of muscle, blood, and bone."

He paused, plopped down on a bench seat

and buried his head in his hands. "Jake had a wife and two young kids back in California. Someone had to tell them. I needed help to get him out of there, but when I looked around, all I saw was another team member kneeling further back on the road, hunched over two still legs. I called out, not sure I made any noise or not. But the man turned his head in my direction."

Austin was on his feet pacing again. "I wasn't certain Sam even recognized me. Tears were streaming down his face and his mouth was open in what must have been a painful wail and in his arms lay a lifeless man. Our friend. Our buddy. Our compadre. Michael 'Skid' Rowe."

The room was quiet for several minutes as the calmest man she'd ever met struggled for control of what was obviously an open, festering wound.

Austin collapsed to his knees beside her. Nicole opened her arms and cradled him like a small child as tears ran quietly down his cheeks. She stroked his silky, thick hair and hummed a lullaby she sang to Libby when nothing else worked.

Evidently he sniffled. "This was what I wanted to do in Iraq, but we had to get out there. The SEALs spent millions training me how to react in a crises. I lifted Skid over my shoulder and hooked an arm with Sam. Mozart grabbed The Snake. Demon ran point. And we all got out of there. But for us that was the end."

Nicole took a breath, glad the tale was over. Grateful he'd made it though. But when she opened her eyes, she realized he was still lost in another time and another place.

"They kept me in the infirmary for two days, when all I wanted was to get out and check on Sam. Finally, they released me. Four hours. It took four hours to find him at the back of a Quonset hut, staring unseeing into the desert. I knelt beside him. One hundred-thirty degrees outside and his hands were ice cold."

Nicole couldn't bear his sorrow. She had to touch him, hold him, protect him from his memories. She took his hand in hers. He swallowed and rallied.

He wiped his eyes with the back of his hand. "Sorry to be so maudlin."

"What happened to Sam?" she prodded gently. "How did you get him to speak?"

"I talked to him."

She squeezed his hand.

A long ragged sigh followed, before Austin said, "I asked, 'Did he say anything before he died?'" His face crumbled.

This time Nicole stroked his face, drying the tears with her thumb.

"Sam choked up and could barely get the words out. Skid's last request. 'Tell my family and my girl, Cricket, that I was brave.'" Austin's voice dropped to a rough whisper. "Sam told me…." He stopped almost unable to go on, but in a voice raw with hurt, anger, and pain, he said, "Sam promised Skid, he'd tell his family he'd been a hero."

She pulled him to her and held him tight. He accepted her offer of comfort, grounding himself in the touch of a friend. "Skid smiled that goofy grin, closed his eyes and said, 'a hero' as though Sam's saying it made all the difference."

Tears streamed down her face. He had shed all of his tears, but she hadn't. They clung together until he pulled away. She let him go, sensing he needed both physical and emotional distance.

He rolled to his feet, stepped to the closet and removed his bag from the top shelf. He dug out two bottles of water and handed one to her. In the bathroom he wet some paper towels so she could wipe her face. She accepted the wet towels noticing he didn't look in her direction.

While she wondered how she could bridge the gap, he busied himself, checking on Lynch again. Both knew it wasn't needed for any other reason than a momentarily cease between them.

She stood and stretched, her body stiff from

the floor. She discarded the paper towels and dug around in the luggage until she found some crackers. He was embarrassed. Big brave SEALs didn't break down. They persevered. She shook her head. But behind their bravery, they were still men who needed to come to grips with the horrors they saw.

He rejoined her and shook off her offer of crackers. She needed to let it go, but still she had to ask, "What happened to Sam?"

Austin shrugged and took a long swig of water before answering. "He went to Missouri, talked to the family and came back."

Talk about a change in attitude. "That isn't all."

He studied her face, his intense blue eyes searching for something. "He lost his swagger, but worse he lost his laugh. In some ways he died along with Skid. Are you finished with the water?"

# Chapter Seventeen

*Somewhere over the Atlantic Ocean*

Austin was stunned he'd told her about Sam. Why did this woman affect him in such a way? He'd told her things he'd never told anybody – ever.

Zack, the team CO, would have boxed his ears. Had he rescued her? No, she'd saved herself. Had he been professional? No, he'd forgotten his job, confided in her, stuttered, stammered, and played kissy face. And if he was honest, the one thing he wanted more than anything was to make love to her.

She'd burrowed under his skin. Sex could exorcise a woman from him. After a wild night or two between the sheets he could move on. But he couldn't allow that. His only hope was that he'd find a way to ease the itch she created.

Nothing about this woman had proved true so far.

He glanced at his watch and tried to figure out how he could survive six more hours of this flight.

Lynch's computer had been password protected in almost every file but the one he had open. Personnel. Austin had downloaded the entire file to his jump drive, but not without a quick perusal of the men he'd encountered in Italy. Mozart's information was brief, factual and didn't mention any of the unusual traits his friend possessed.

His blood had run cold when he'd looked at Charles "Laser-Beam" Ernst, former Army Ranger and sniper.

Unable to sit after his confession, Austin paced the small room. Nicole avoided him. She tidied the area, disposed of trash, washed her hands, and used the facilities. A crash with the distinct sound of breaking glass came from the front room. She jerked open the bathroom door, her lips firmed with determination and her eyes narrow slits.

He gestured with a toss of his head toward the closet as he grabbed his tablet and fell in behind her. He thrust the tablet at her and bent to retrieve his snub nose revolver from his ankle holster.

"He's coming this way, lurching like he's drunk." Nicole clicked the switch at the top of the device. The closet went black.

Austin didn't adjust the louvers out of fear the other man would notice. The sound of a door opening meant Lynch preferred the rear bathroom probably because he didn't bother to close the door. Nicole stood rigidly by Austin's side as the sounds of urine hitting the metal interior of the commode came through loud and clear.

Nice. He was sort of embarrassed for the woman whose delicate sensitivities were probably offended, but then the humor hit him. Lynch peed forever. It was like a bad comedy. In a movie theatre Austin might have laughed out loud. Her arm grazed his. She was chuckling also. She thought this was funny? She was so not what he'd imagined.

The stream slowed then stopped and Lynch lurched noisily into the room. Chairs moved. Austin cautiously adjusted the slats. Nicole leaned into him. He wrapped an arm around her and shifted her position so that her back was plastered to his front allowing her to see.

Lynch sat at the conference table with his forehead pressed against the light wood. For several minutes he half-laid across the table in what appeared to be total exhaustion before reaching for a triangular piece of equipment in the middle. He fiddled with the gadget, and the screen on the wall flickered to life. A face appeared. Austin didn't recognize the younger man's hard features, but he could always spot a warrior and this man fit the bill.

"You look like hell. What happened?"

Austin curled an arm firmly around Nicole's

waist to keep her anchored to him. "Two-way television," he whispered in her ear, his cheek nestled in her short hair. Her head nodded, the barest of moves.

Lynch rubbed the back of his neck like it hurt.

"You okay?"

"No. I'm coming down with something, maybe the Norovirus or the flu or something. I feel like shit." His gravelly voice sounded like that of a dying man.

Just how many sleeping pills had Nicole put in his drink? She exhaled softly, shifting her weight to rest more in Austin's arms, a pleasurable sensation.

"Where are you now?" The man on the television asked.

"On my way home. Have CJ meet me at the airport with a car around six."

The face plastered across the fifty inch screen bobbed. "It's all over the news that the Senator's wife drowned. Too bad."

Austin bit back a grin. Nicole stiffened. Automatically he rubbed her arms to offer her comfort. He raised his hand and flashed four fingers at her three times to remind her of the breathing exercises he'd shown her in the hotel room. She relaxed as her breathing calmed her.

Lynch picked at his eyebrows, a move that

drew Austin's attention to the abundant black
hairs that ran in a severe line over his dark eyes.
"Cleves with the FBI called. I'm meeting with
him as soon as I get back. Seems the Senator's
under investigation. Apparently he liked to
smack the little woman around. The FBI's
investigating why it wasn't reported by a
hospital or an ER."

Austin quickly placed a hand across her lips
to keep a gasp from coming out. She shook her
head to get him to remove his fingers. She was
tougher than he'd imagined.

"How are you coming on finding the wife's
baby?" Lynch asked.

"The kid went over the border at San Diego
with a woman named Elena Vasquez. Worked
for the wife's family years before. Her neighbor
gave us a forwarding address in Buenos Aires
that belongs to her family. We're confident she'll
show up there within the next day or two. Do
you want me to send someone ahead to find out
if the family knows anything?"

Nicole straightened and he tightened his
grip. Shudders racked her frail skeleton and in
the dim light he could see her biting her lips to
keep from crying out.

"Argentina?" Lynch shook his head. "Why
would she send a special-needs kid who requires
constant medical attention to a country without

adequate health care?"

"Fear. Maybe the Senator liked to smack around more than the little woman, who, by-the-way is a real looker."

"Yeah, so far she's nothing like Layton described her. Someone jumped off the cruise ship in a dry suit just before the ship lost power. Mozart was convinced it was her. He's usually got good instincts. Check that news story out. Make sure they've got the facts right."

"Gotcha. You want me to contact the Senator about location of the child?"

"Not yet. Let's hear what the FBI knows first."

"You might want to catch some shut eye while you've got time. Maybe you can sleep this thing off."

"Yeah, I think I will."

The screen went black. Lynch lowered his head to the table and appeared to doze off for a few minutes. Silently, Austin closed the louvers so all the doors would look the same. They waited in the dark until they heard a bumping noise some distance away. He clicked on the screen of his tablet to see Lynch had returned to the front room and was now slumped in the recliner, a new drink in his hand and the end of the Wild Turkey in his glass.

"Bottoms ups," he whispered in Nicole's ear.

As though programmed, Lynch took a swig.

◈

Nicole had limited success at getting comfortable. She sat cross-legged, trying to minimize her floor space to give Austin more room. Her mind whirled. Those men knew where Libby was, which meant it was only a question of time before Linus knew. If her husband believed she was dead, he might not pursue Libby. But the guy in the other room was a bull dog. He wouldn't give up.

Her world shattered. For months she'd believed if she could get away from Linus she'd have weeks to get to a safe location. What a fool she'd been. Austin found her in hours. Linus would know where Libby was before another day passed.

Could she get word to Elena? Tell her to hide out – somewhere isolated – except Libby was not a child who could live off the grid. Nicole hung her head in her hands overwhelmed by the failure of her plan.

Warm fingers stroked her hair then left her. Glancing up she realized he was texting. His thumbs moved lightning fast. He dropped to a crouching position and whispered, "Do you have the Argentina address or phone number?"

Numbly she nodded and recited both from memory. He tried to help. Libby was only a child. An innocent pawn in the power struggle between husband and wife. Nicole would sign her own death certificate and return to Linus if it meant her niece was safe.

"I have a friend in South America. Former SEAL. A guy named Hooch. I'm asking him to watch for Elena and the child. See if he can offer any help. He's a resourceful guy – a good man to have on our side. Nothing's happened yet. Have faith." He squeezed her hand.

Austin came armed with a plan. Yes, he'd come to her rescue, but since the dawn of time knights had been saving the princess, battling through walls of thorns, slaying dragons and other mythical creatures, expecting once he reached her that their troubles would end. The hero had saved the girl and they would live happily ever after.

How many men were prepared for a different ending, where happily ever after wasn't even a possibility?

Through it all he was unfazed, going about his duties like this was a normal day. In the closet, lit only by the light of his cell phone, she studied his calm face. For him, this was a normal day. Today he rescued Nicole. And Libby. Tomorrow it would be a different woman and perhaps another child.

He leaned over her and opened the louvered door a few inches to allow a cool breeze to stir the air. His scent filled the room. She inhaled, trying to take in his masculine essence.

Even though she'd only known him for a few days, there was something about him that relaxed her. His quiet alertness kept her fears and worries at bay, allowing her to think, to see past the immediate danger. Libby would be safe. Austin would see to it.

As a child, she'd hugged an overstuffed teddy bear when the monsters in the closet threatened. But Austin was no harmless stuffed animal.

She was aware of him as a man – a very desirable man. All her life she'd been surrounded by men who saw themselves as above the law. Not this man. He did remarkable, brave things – things that would have most men crowing and strutting, but he was humble. And kind.

She'd been sitting for too long. Her legs were cramped. She refused to complain, but Austin with one eye on his monitor was aware of her every thought.

"Stretch out." He shifted to give her room, extending his own legs as well, he set aside the tablet and turned his full attention to her. "You cold?"

She shook her head. Not with him hovering

over her. She briefly wondered what that little groove was called that ran from the nose to his mouth. His was deep and his lips were sharply defined. Yesterday, he'd been clean shaven. Today he sported a faint growth of beard that would tickle if she ran her palm across his cheek. When that thought jumped into her brain, her hand felt compelled to follow through. Touching him thrilled her. She raised her gaze and swore the dim light reflected flames in his eyes. A shiver ran up her back.

Her breath came in short pants as though oxygen was at premium. The pounding in her chest was loud enough she was sure he could hear the repetitive fast-paced thumping. She wanted his closeness – longed for it. He remained suspended over her. Tension crackled between them.

When she couldn't stand one more second, he lowered his head and nibbled her lips. Not enough. Not nearly enough. She snaked an arm around his shoulders and drew him closer, dismissing any warnings her brain screamed with the single thought that this was only a kiss. Or actually a series of kisses.

She wanted him. Pure and simple. Well, maybe not so pure. His body was a temptation that she longed to sate this craving that ate at her. She stretched beneath him and he followed her movement with his own. A murmur of contentment rumbled out of her chest.

"Shhh," he whispered. "No sexy little sounds."

He squeezed her nipple and had his weight not been on top of her she would have leapt up. Where she would have gone she had no idea.

He rose and unbuttoned his shirt, taking his time while his gaze scanned her face. Her brain emerged from its fog long enough to discern his intent. Was he waiting to see if she'd stop him? That wasn't going to happen. Her only wish was that he'd speed up.

He pulled her t-shirt over her head, and she half-lifted off the floor to help. "Why do you wear such plain underwear?"

Her cheeks heated in the darkened space. "In the beginning to keep my husband from touching me, but he hated my body. I was too skinny and unappealing."

Austin's eyes crinkled in amusement. "You're kidding, right?"

"I wish."

"That man's a bigger fool than I thought." He lowered his head. She could smell the clean scent of odorless shampoo as he kissed the tops of her breasts. "Sit up."

He unfastened her back-hook bra with one hand, impressing her with his knowledge of women's undergarments, then unwrapped her ace bandage before unzipping her pants. She lay back and shifted her hips to remove them. He settled on top of her running his large warm hand from her knees, over her thigh, hips and ribcage to clasp a breast.

"You're still dressed."

"I took off my shirt." His arm band tattoo ran up and encircled his shoulder. She longed for a closer look, but moving would mean he'd stop playing with her nipple.

"You're still wearing pants." She pouted. Oh, Lord. She hadn't flirted since high school. And she hadn't been naked at the time.

"You make me want things I shouldn't. I've lost my mind, clinging to my pants seems like a good idea. This way, things won't go too quickly."

She sensed a hidden caveat. If she put on the brakes, he'd still have control. He was protecting her and would do whatever she asked. She smiled, trying for light-heartedness. "I'm not changing my mind."

His lips met hers and whatever thoughts she had were sucked out of her brain. His rough-hewn fingers tortured her breast, pinching her nipple. Her impulse was to moan. Restraining herself proved difficult even when she clamped her teeth together. Her body thought that anything that felt this good needed to be celebrated as loudly as possible. This wasn't her. She was sedate, mature.

Her fingers danced across his skin memorizing the dips and bundles of his muscles. He growled in her ear, low and deep then lowered his head to her nipples and suckled. Blood pulsed. She arched, demanding more. Cool air circled her wet nipples when he raised his head. Muttered cursing should have made her laugh had she not been clinging to the edge of her control.

He jerked open his jean shorts and tugged them down his legs. "Can you come quietly?"

Could she? She nodded, knowing she would make it happen. In the past week she'd proved she could do the impossible. He fumbled in his pocket and withdrew a single foil-wrapped condom. Quickly he sheathed himself.

He raised her legs and settled between them, spreading her wide. She couldn't wait, lunging for him with grasping hands.

"If your ribs hurt, let me know."

Never had she been involved with a man who made her wild with need. Newfound freedom went to her head. She was having a one-night stand with the sexiest man she'd ever met. She longed to tell him how she felt, but the words froze in her throat.

Instead she closed her eyes, tilted her head backward, and clung to him. Needing him to keep her safe and make her feel feminine and wanted. How long had it been since someone, anyone had wanted her? How long had it been since a man had seen her as anything but an empty-headed blonde?

# Chapter Eighteen

"Nicole." The guttural word he uttered in the silence of the closet was wrenched from his gut. Words were magical. They had power. He'd known it since childhood.

The one single word, her name, had danced in his brain and now morphed into a thought. Like a thread of smoke it circled and obscured competing ideas. It consumed him becoming an addictive action. Having her once would never be enough. No matter where she went. No matter where she hid. He would be there with her because he could no longer let her go.

The action became an obsessive prayer that devoured him.

Austin slumped over her, grasping for breath, trying to clear his head.

From fifteen to thirty-five he had sex with a wide variety of willing participants - mostly fun-seeking women who hadn't wanted an attachment any more than he. Nicole was different. Sex with her had been terrifying. It changed him.

Now – during the afterglow – was when he left, usually giving some feeble excuse and slipping out the door. Unless his adrenaline was still high from a dangerous op. Then he might spend the night going without sleep for hours until his energy was depleted. But sleep? He never slept with women.

He didn't cuddle. He only kissed because women expected it. Kissing Nicole wasn't a chore. Her kiss anchored him. Making love to her colored in all the black pieces in his soul.

*Shake this off.*

He eased his weight to his forearms. "You okay?"

"Oh, yeah." Her voice held the rich quality of a satisfied cat.

His lips quirked in male satisfaction. "What about your ribs?"

"Really, they're fine."

He needed to move, to get physically away from her. To clear his head. "I need to check on Lynch."

His muscles refused to act, betraying him. His mind screamed in panic. He lowered his head to her shoulder, seeking control.

Her cool fingers touched the back of his neck and slid into his hair. He never wanted to go. The words he left unsaid, hung in the air. He loved her. Love had kicked him in the gut and wrestled him to the ground. And now he lay hog-tied, afraid to stay – unable to leave.

He stretched, turning the tablet on, without unhinging from the woman beneath him. The screen showed Lynch still sleeping. They'd been in the air for hours with a long flight still ahead of them. He lowered his head and kissed her again as his mind devised ways to pass the time.

"I have to go to the bathroom," she said as she pushed against his shoulders.

He lifted his body off hers as he withdrew. Something was wrong. His fingers gripped the sticky condom. This wasn't good. He reared back to sit on his heels. The condom had split.

"Nicole, I'm sorry… " he began.

She quickly took in the situation. "It's okay. The timing's not right for pregnancy." She patted his cheek as she slid out from under him. "Really," she whispered. "It's not a problem."

Granted getting her pregnant was the big worry, but lots of other things could occur. When they were safe, he'd insist she go to the doctor and make sure she was okay.

*Washington DC*

Landing a jet of this size should have been smoother. The plane bounced and lurched forward as the pilots braked hard. Austin rolled to protect Nicole from crashing into the closet doors. Lynch was awake.

Austin rose to his feet and slid the door open far enough to see the night sky. His watch dial glowed three minutes to midnight, but he'd set it on Rome's time. His cell phone showed three minutes before six. Buildings weren't visible to clue him into where they were, but he hoped they'd landed at Dulles or Reagan, not at Andrews Air Force Base

Nicole shifted. He offered a hand to help her stand. She whispered, "As soon as he and the pilots are off, I'll redress and gather our stuff."

He shook his head. "It may be a while before we get off. We've got to make sure the hangar is empty."

"Good. That will give me time to tidy up, so he won't know he had passengers even after the fact. Am I still pregnant?"

He tugged her to him and kissed her lightly. "This is DC, honey. The most likely place you'll be recognized. You still need to play the part."

Both watched the screen and followed the other man's every move. Lynch clasped his head in his hands as though he was in pain. When he released his head, he picked up the empty bottle of Wild Turkey and eyed it with suspicion. Austin tensed. Lynch hadn't gotten to be where he was by being stupid. The fact he was sniffing the bottle was worrisome. Yes, they were safely on the ground and out of Italy, but this could still blow up in their faces.

Nicole's head rested against his chest

blocking her from seeing the screen. Austin was glad he didn't have to soothe her as well. It was enough for him to worry for the two of them. The plane came to a halt and Austin slid the door open to see if he could locate their position – without luck.

Lynch repacked his laptop and slung his duffle over his shoulder, but he kept the empty bottle under his arm. One of the pilots emerged from the cockpit and prepared the plane for his passenger to exit.

Austin crawled from the closet to peer out the window. The pilot followed Lynch to the tarmac. The two men were in a heated conversation with Lynch gesturing, using the bottle as a pointer toward the plane.

Austin leapt into action.

"Come quickly," he told her.

Nicole hurried out of the closet and Austin kicked their blankets and pillows into a dark heap under the clothes.

Her eyes were wide, anxious determination written on her face as she waited for his instruction. He hurried her to the bench seating that had held the pillows and blankets underneath and lifted the seat. "Get in."

She laid face down in the small opening and he laid a blanket over her, before closing the seating. He ran to the closet with the copier and squatted down next to the furthest wall. In the seconds that followed he heard footsteps and the opening of the closet door, followed by the door to the copier closet. Light from the room lit up his hiding place, but he doubted the pilot searched in-depth. The door closed almost as quickly as it opened.

"What are you doing?" A second male voice asked.

"Lynch is getting more paranoid than ever. I'm checking to see if anybody else is on the plane."

"What the… Why does he think that?"

"Who knows? I didn't argue with him. You know how he gets when someone disagrees with him. Told him I'd check, so I'm checking."

Another door latched which Austin assumed was the bathroom. "Nothing."

"Let's get out of here. I don't know about you, but I could use a beer."

"Call the cleaning crew. Have them get out here in the morning. The plane needs a good going over. One closet is full of junk and there's a funky odor."

Nicole concentrated on her breathing. In. Out. In. Out. Her heart pounded in her chest as she cautioned herself not to panic. Austin had known what to do. If they'd caught her, what could she have said or done?

The lid lifted and the blanket was lifted. "You okay?" Austin wrapped a hand around her upper arm to help her up.

The only light that filtered through the windows was from the fluorescents that lit the hanger's interior. The bay door was open, showing a black sky with low-to-the-ground lights twinkling in the distance. She had no idea what time her body thought it was, but the length of the day closed in on her. Her knees sagged, and she clutched the back of the seat cover for support.

Austin snaked an arm around her waist adding his support as his gaze searched her face.

"I'm fine." She gave a weak smile.

"We came close to being caught." His frown told her he knew something he hadn't told her. "Lynch knows he was drugged. He took the bottle with him." His voice was composed which Nicole recognized as his fighting stance. Unlike most people who went to hysterical when faced with a problem, Austin settled into an alert calmness which in turn reassured those around him – particularly her.

How different from Linus. When he was worried, her tension ratcheted up to match his. Austin's belief in his ability to handle the situation made it easier not to worry. Her one big idea to drug Lynch had been a disaster.

She bit her lips unsure whether to apologize. "What does that mean?"

"We need to get out of here." He grinned. "Don't worry. We're almost home."

Home. Where was home? To her, Libby was home.

"Are the pilots gone?"

"Yeah, I haven't seen anybody else, but that doesn't mean we're alone. Can you dress in the dark?"

She nodded. "I'll clean up the closet, too. Have you heard anything from your friend in South America?"

"He's headed to Buenos Aires and will get in touch with me as soon as he knows something. I'm grabbing the cameras from the front room."

Twenty minutes later they were ready to go. Austin was bundled in a coat, scarf, and hat. Nicole wore a hoody and sported her baby bump.

"As soon as you hit the ground, don't wait for me to close the door. Move quickly outside the building, keep your head down, and stand in the shadows. I'll catch up in a minute."

He gave her a quick kiss. She longed to scream in frustration. When would this end? Would she ever be safe or would she spend the rest of her life looking over her shoulder?

Shame flashed over her. This path had been

her choice, and she had no one to blame but herself.

"Smile, beautiful." He reassured her, his lips curling into an easy smile. "We're on American soil."

She leveled a dubious look in his direction, not sure that being in America would help.

# Chapter Nineteen

*Washington DC*

Hiram Lynch's worry stone had been getting a workout for the past two hours. Even now as the town car inched through the bumper-to-bumper DC traffic he rubbed the stone nestled in his pocket. The biting January night air poured in from the open backseat window where Hiram sat gazing at lights reflected in the wet pavement. CJ, his driver, his long-time companion and friend, drove in silence as Hiram mentally rehashed the worthless meeting he'd been dragged back from Italy to attend.

Deputy Chief Aaron Cleves's disrespect had bordered on the intolerable. He had no pertinent information to impart that Lynch didn't already know or suspect. The Senator slapped his wife around, so what? He paid for it. Look at her jet-setting lifestyle. Vail. Lake Powell. Lake Forest. That was some expensive real estate. The Senator's private relationship with his wife hardly needed an investigation.

No, Lynch had been called to Washington for a fishing expedition. Big waste of time he never ratted out his clients. The ache that had pounded his temples for the past hour had abated with the help of ibuprofen.

He laid his head against the leather headrest and closed his eyes. Nothing about Layton's case was turning out the way he'd hoped.

Wearily he opened his eyes to check his phone which, between the flight and the meeting, had been off for several hours. A video feed appeared on his screen. He pushed the arrow and watched the door on his plane open. Two people descended – a very pregnant brunette whose face was obscured by a gray hood and sun-glasses despite the time of day and a taller male hidden by a plaid wool scarf and fedora. The woman immediately disappeared from the camera view, but the man operated the plane door quickly and efficiently. In less than fifteen seconds there was no indication at all that the intruders had deplaned.

Relief mixed with anger poured through him. He knew it. He'd been drugged. His teammates claimed he'd slept with one eye open. Never heavy. Never for hours on end. Despite his age of forty-one, he wasn't slipping.

If he hadn't insisted on video surveillance, no one would have suspected anything at all. Faces on the video weren't visible, but his instincts told him his passengers were the not-so-dead Nicole Layton and Austin Stevens. Had the Senator failed to mention his wife was several months pregnant? No wonder they hadn't spotted her in Rome. Overlooking a pregnant woman in a crowd would have been easy.

Well played. This was the second time the Stevens brothers had interfered. They were becoming quite the problem.

How was Aaron Cleves involved? He had to be in on it with that trumped up call. His jaw ached. Automatically Hiram did the exercises his dentist had recommended to keep the TMJ at bay.

He despised failure and dreaded having to call the Senator whose only request had been to find a dead wife. This situation had one possibility of being salvaged. He'd killed before. He could do it again. This time he'd make it two for the price of one.

"CJ, what'd you find out about the news story? Any truth to it?"

A hand adjusted the rear-view mirror. The heavily lidded black eyes blinked as he adjusted to the darkness of the rear seat. "Still checking. Why? You think it's a cover up?" CJ's words were slow, like he struggled to decide on each one, but Hiram knew that to underestimate the man was a major mistake most people didn't have a second chance to make.

He snatched his cell phone from his jacket pocket and punched in the number of one of his

Portland operatives. The man answered on the first ring.

"Get out to Portland International Airport. I want you to watch incoming flights that originated out of DC, even if there was a stop-over in the middle. Send someone else to watch the homes of the Stevens Securities brothers. I'm sending you a video of the couple I want followed. This guy is good. Don't lose him."

⚙

*Denver International Airport*
*Thursday, January 19th*

As the 747 began its descent into the Denver Airport, swirling snowflakes danced in the lights delighting the passengers, who responded with "oohs" and "ahs". The ground below them was a solid white blanket decorated with shiny bling in the form of red, yellow, and green lights. The concrete runway was a patchwork quilt of white and gray. The yellow directional arrows had been reduced to tiny dashes. Like the other passengers, Nicole peered out the window.

"We have received permission to land and will be on the ground in minutes. Please remain seated with your seatbelts firmly fastened."

More protected but less exciting than the previous landing which involved the full-length of Austin's body securing her to the ground.

She stared at the snow that sparkled in the lights of the airport. The tires bounced, rolled, bounced, rolled, then the entire plane skidded sideways. She grabbed Austin's hand and squeezed. The plane corrected its path allowing the passengers to sigh in collective relief.

When the big plane taxied to the gate and the engines shut down, everyone burst into applause, whistles, and cheers. The elation continued until those with connecting flights realized no other planes were leaving until the storm let up some time tomorrow.

Airport officials used the word 'lucky' in repetitive sentences. Lucky was never a word Nicole associated with herself, but she was grateful to not have encountered weather as a major deterrent in her battle to escape her marriage. She walked the long corridor of concourse gates while Austin sought isolation in an alcove to phone his brother. An overhead television screen flashed a photo of Linus and herself with the words 'breaking news' as a banner headline. Nicole moved closer to hear the report as a photo of the Costa Concordia Cruise ship lay on its side in the shallow waters of Giglio Island filled the screen. While the story was supposed to be about her death notice, the focus was on the ship's problems. The only mention of Nicole Layton was that she'd had the privilege of being married to the senior senator from Illinois.

Disgusted she went in search of Austin.

"Everything happens for a reason." Her sister used to say. "The sooner one figures out the reason, the sooner they can move on."

Austin had asked why she didn't get an abortion. That was why. Beth had a lesson to learn. Nicole didn't agree with her philosophy and she didn't agree with her solution to the problem, but she now knew why it was easier to kill yourself than to suck it up until the end.

As she walked, her thoughts drifted to her mother who had moved to Fort Collins, a small town nearby. A sigh escaped her lips. She didn't understand her mother. Beth had. In many ways Beth and their mother saw eye-to-eye. After her father's arrest the two had formed a unified pact. Nicole considered herself an outsider and spent most of her teenage years counting the days until she turned eighteen and could move out on her own. Even living apart, nothing she did met with her mother's approval including making a home for Libby.

But then she'd married Linus – a senator with prestige and money. And suddenly the sun came out. All the old fights were forgotten. For the first time in her life, she'd been the favorite. When her marriage revealed its true colors and

Linus broke her arm, her mother had quizzed her on what she'd done to anger him.

They never understood each other and that hadn't changed. But her mother loved her in her own way, and she deserved to know her daughter was not dead.

Nicole believed in signs. And the fact they were stopped in Denver and couldn't get on another plane was a definite sign. Every important document in connection with her marriage had been sent to her mother's house. When Nicole planned to disappear in Europe she believed she hadn't needed the paperwork. Now with Libby in jeopardy, fate was telling her that whatever was in that paperwork might save her life.

Austin grinned as she approached, then frowned. "What's worrying you?"

Would he stop her? A muscular arm stole around her waist as though he sensed her concern. Nicole shifted her weight to lean against Austin, welcoming his warmth. No. He'd do everything he could to help her.

"What did Travis know?" She laid her head against his shoulder seeking comfort.

"Problems in Portland," he spoke into her ear in that toneless voice he'd perfected that created intimacy between them.

*What's new?* Nicole bit back the bitter retort

out of fear Austin would feel the necessity of reassuring her even further.

"The boat dock is being watched. He thinks we should look for transportation other than the next flight."

"The boat dock?"

"We own a dock of houseboats, eight in all. I live in one, Travis and Abby live in another, employees and family rent out the rest."

Nicole pivoted her body, liking the way his eyes lit up when he spoke of his home. "If you didn't mind, since we are stuck here, we could visit my mother."

His blue eyes studied hers for a moment. "Tonight? Where is she?"

"Fort Collins. Less than a hundred miles from here, but morning would be better."

He nodded accepting her words without argument. "Let's rent a car and grab a hotel room."

It couldn't be that easy. "What if someone's watching her house?

"Then we'll keep driving or we'll sneak in the back door. There is no problem we won't be able to solve together."

A small smile crept to her lips. When had a man ever treated her like a partner? "You are too good to me."

He stopped, turning toward her, surprise in

his eyes. "You don't think you deserve someone to be good you?"

Her mind scrambled for an answer. She hadn't meant it the way it came out. She wasn't pathetic. "It's just unusual."

He shook his head. "If you were mine, you'd never think that again." He paused as the words he spoke hung in the air, a slight panicked look in his eyes. "Ignore that. We're both tired. Let's grab a rental car and find a hotel room before they are all gone."

Nicole forced her feet to move, but all the time wondering how a woman was supposed to ignore words like 'if you were mine'?

Snow fell in big fat flakes. Traffic on I-25 north had slowed to a crawl. The windshield wipers slapped back and forth smearing the wetness. Tires had no traction, and while Austin controlled their car, others slipped and slid all over the road.

A lit motel sign complete with a neon vacancy notice had Austin pulling into the parking lot. "Not spectacular but it will do."

Skittishness attacked her. She didn't know how to act around this man that she'd come to count on. The night and the waiting bedroom made her uncertain. There was no reason not to have sex, was there? The closet had been intimate, but cramped. The self-imposed need for silence had heightened the tension, but what would Austin be like when he let loose? Under that tough in-control exterior was a wild man that she'd only caught a bit of rough edges. Her nerves tingled with anticipation.

"Hungry?"

*For food? No.*

She shook her head as he unlocked the door to the first floor room. She wished she owned a sexy nightgown, but like hats and white gloves, negligees had disappeared from the American woman's wardrobe.

"Do you want to shower first?" he asked as he tossed their bag on one of the two queen beds.

Once again he deferred to her which wasn't at all what she wanted. They wouldn't be together forever, but for now she wanted him - anyway she could have him.

Stepping closer she circled her arms around his waist, annoyed by the baby bump that created distance. "I want to shower with you."

A short choked laugh followed. "Let's go then. We need to schedule some time to sleep tonight."

At her raised eyebrow, he added with a wink and a grin, "at least thirty minutes" making her heart pound loudly in her chest.

Her clothes clung to her as she worked the

stubborn buttons through the holes of the skirt and blouse that covered the pregnancy bump. Austin lifted the weight off her shoulders and hung it in the closet, putting away a slice of her life.

Glancing in the mirror her reflection surprised her. The brunette that stared back wasn't the Senator's adoring wife or her mother's rebellious daughter. Nor was she the mousy librarian. A few weeks earlier she believed the only way to escape her husband was to run to a different country and live a different life. To always hide in the shadows constantly looking over one shoulder. The woman who stared back at her in the mirror had courage, strength, and could face her problems. If there was one thing the past several days had taught her was that she had options.

Mindlessly, she removed her clothes as she considered her next course of action. She was lost in her own thoughts until she realized Austin was toeing off his shoes. She found herself transfixed as he tugged the gray t-shirt over his head. His chest looked like a muscled ad for a gym.

"You, too, could have this body working out only twenty minutes a day." Some television announcer would say while selling an outrageously priced piece of gym equipment.

His body wasn't exclusive. It could be had by anyone willing to undergo the discipline. Austin's uniqueness lay in his heart. She'd never met another man like him and doubted there were two.

He shimmied out of his jeans and tossed them onto the bed, giving her a view of his left buttock cheek and another tattoo. This one was a snarling three-headed sea monster.

She touched the faded ink. "What is this?"

He jumped slightly at her touch. "What an eighteen-year-old thinks is badass."

She tilted her head studying the design as she one-handedly unwrapped the ace bandage circling her chest. "Three heads for the three brothers?"

"Yep. Water for SEAL wannabes. Stupid, huh?"

"A commitment to a promise is never stupid. Doesn't that tat represent you and your brothers honoring your stepfather by becoming SEALs?"

His startled look told her she'd guessed right.

"You've put the best possible spin on it. Although I doubt I was that noble at eighteen."

She unfastened her bra and slid her panties to the ground making a mental note to purchase sexier underwear the next time she had an opportunity. This was a man who'd made love to hundreds, maybe thousands of women, but he needed seducing. He was so busy caring for everyone else that nobody nursed his wounds. The first thing she wanted to do was slap a little sense into him.

"Don't be ridiculous. At eleven you didn't kill your father for revenge. Your goal was to protect your family. You may have done some dumb things growing up, but you were born with a higher sense of honor than any man I've ever known."

It wouldn't have mattered if she'd been standing on the far side of the moon. He crossed the separation between then, folding her into his arms within seconds. He kissed his way across her jaw until their lips met. And she knew in her heart leaving him would be the hardest thing she would ever have to do.

The bed appeared behind her knees and they collapsed onto it. He kissed her with a desperation born of longing. Until now sex had been superficial, but she'd struck a chord in his soul. The blood in her veins pulsed and pounded with a rhythm as old as time.

If she'd been wearing clothes he would have torn them off as frantic as his desire was. She was desperate for him and didn't need preamble. Every growl, moan, and pant pushed her higher. He couldn't move fast enough. Both scrambled for the fastest fit. Within seconds he was pumping into her. But she met every thrust with one of her own. His caveman technique excited her to the point that when he collapsed, she flipped him on his back, climbed on top and took over the direction. Her hips working like a piston, slamming her sex against his. She came and then came again.

It was the most satisfying and most depressing sex in her life. In order to be safe she would have to leave. At this moment in time she rather die than leave. Her body collapsed.

Exhaustion, restless dreams, and insatiable desire had her sleeping in fitful spurts. The first time they made love was wild, the second was sweet.

The third time he reached for her, tears welled in her eyes. The blackout curtains made the room pitch black, but as attuned as they were to each other, he immediately asked, "What's wrong?"

"Nothing."

"Tell me." He stroked his thumb across her cheek wiping away the tears that had leaked out.

This was it. She had to speak. "I can't do this." She raised her arms to touch him but he'd shifted away from her.

Rising he sat on the edge of the bed and

grabbed his jeans. "You don't have to. I won't force myself on you."

"Force yourself on me?" She sat up. "What are you talking about?"

The light next to the bed came on as he pulled on his jeans, carefully avoiding looking at her. "What are you talking about?" He re-asked her question emphasizing the word you.

She'd hurt his feelings. Despite her jumbled thoughts, she had to explain this so that it made sense. "I want to walk in the sun."

"Okaaay." Uncertainty laced the one word he drew out.

She started again. "All my life I've been afraid. I never confronted any situation. I've avoided men, commitment and relationships. And what has it gotten me? One rotten marriage. Certainly not happiness. I'm through running."

He stared at her as though she had grown a second head. This wasn't going the way she wanted at all. "Austin, I want those things with you."

"What things with me?" His face changed as he put together the pieces. "You want to stay with me? What about Layton?"

"I'm going to divorce him."

Austin sat on the edge of the bed with a bewildered look on his face. Granted it was three in the morning, but she'd hoped for a more excited response than this.

"Your husband is not a man to forgive and forget. If he knows where you are, you will never be safe. And what about Libby?"

"Libby and I come as a package deal. So if that turns you off, you need to tell me now. And as for Linus, we'll work it out. I've been told that together we can solve any problem."

Slowly a smile lit his gloriously handsome face. "Not want Libby? How can I not want a child you care about? But you're right. We are an undefeatable team, but you've only known me for a week. When this is over, you'll want some time to sort out your feelings. I can't promise you much, but I will be waiting."

# Chapter Twenty

*Friday, January 20th*
*Ft. Collins, Colorado*

In a written report Austin would later describe Mercedes Bloggett's neighborhood as a meticulously groomed, upscale housing development. Personally he found it pretentious. Each house staked its territory behind security gates and iron fences. Nicole pointed to a white house with southern plantation columns and a sprawling front yard. The street was empty of cars, people or movement. Not an area where children climbed trees or built snowmen.

He found it strangely comforting that this pile of bricks and mortar had never been her home. Her background had indicated a solid middle class upbringing with homes nicer than those of his childhood, but not isolated and cold.

With the fifth husband her mother had achieved her financial goals. But the one thing he knew for certain was that money did not shield anyone from pain.

He pulled up the long driveway and parked near the half-moon ornate brick steps that led to the leaded-glass double front door. Despite Nicole's need to be here, she didn't look eager to leave the car. For a few minutes she didn't move, staring straight ahead at the curved driveway and snow covered bushes, while she appeared to be having an internal war with her thoughts. Then she flashed a smile that reminded him of a toothpaste ad, squared her shoulders and opened the door.

Somewhere in the night, Nicole had found direction. In that moment she'd chosen him. Hours ago, he'd rejoiced, but now apprehension set in, knowing it was merely a matter of time before she realized she'd committed the cliché of falling for her rescuer.

The baby bump was packed in the trunk. This trip had held some surprises for him. Despite her appearance, Nicole had been pretty low maintenance, needing nothing more than to finger comb her hair and apply a little makeup.

This morning after she'd showered, she'd fluffed, spindle, and folded her face until evidence of the Senator's wife had re-emerged. Even now, standing in the snow at the front, she fussed with her hair while waiting for someone to answer.

Austin positioned himself behind her and slightly apart. He'd expected an older version of the Senator's wife to answer the door and wasn't disappointed. He quickly did the math in his head. The woman had to be mid-fifties, but she scarcely looked older than her daughter. He sensed bad blood between them based on comments Nicole made, but he wasn't prepared for her words of welcome to be, "What did you do to your hair?"

"Hello, mother," Nicole said, leaning forward to exchange air kisses.

"I knew you weren't dead." Mercedes wrapped an arm around her daughter's shoulders and ushered her through the door. "Come inside. Your guard can wait in the car."

He choked back a laugh. This woman was a piece of work. He waited wanting to see Nicole's reaction. Her feet froze.

"Austin is not my guard. He's the reason I'm alive."

Mercedes looked over her shoulder at the man she'd already dismissed and slowly ran her gaze over him and, not surprisingly, found him wanting. "Forgive me. Do come in. Would you like some coffee?"

"Yes, please."

He trouped down the hall following the duo. The cloying smell of floral air freshener run amuck had him holding his breath. Big decorator rooms flashed by as they headed to the open kitchen. Out of habit he checked the yard for potential dangers as he listened to the conversation.

"Gerry's doctor says he has to lose twenty pounds so I don't have any pastries to offer."

Nicole took a seat at the large island. "What about cocoa?"

"Really, Nicole, I'd have thought you'd overgrown your chocolate obsession." But she opened a cabinet. "I only have instant."

Austin grinned. *So Nicole was a fan of chocolate.*

Mercedes placed a cup of water in the microwave and measured cocoa for the cup. "If you keep this up, you're going to end up fat. Then nobody will want you."

Austin almost choked. If anything Nicole could stand to gain weight. She was thin to the point of fragile.

"No marshmallows?"

A long suffering sigh followed as Mercedes produced an unopened bag of mini-marshmallows and heaped them into the cocoa.

She placed the mug in front of her daughter before pouring coffee into cup and placing it on the kitchen table across the room from where Nicole sat. How had she mastered subtly when her mother was an obvious train wreck?

Nicole stood, picked up her cup, and crossed the floor to the table to take the seat next to his drink. "Meet Austin Stevens. He owns a security firm in Portland, Oregon. He saved my life."

Austin and Mercedes spared the barest nods for each other. Nicole's eyes sparkled. She held the cup in front of her mouth hiding what Austin suspected was a grin of amusement. Mercedes opened a package of cookies, put them on a plate and set them on the table before pouring a second cup of coffee.

"Your father called this morning. He was distraught over the news of your death."

Austin found it interesting that Mercedes didn't ask one word about how her daughter's life had been in jeopardy.

Nicole's expression was unreadable. "But you knew before the news story came out. Who told you I was dead?"

"Your husband's office called yesterday. A man, Hiram something, told me you'd drowned. Hiram… Such an unusual name. Old fashioned like the royal princesses. What are their names? Beatrice and Eugenie?"

Austin and Nicole exchanged a look. "What did Hiram say to you?" She asked, keeping her face hidden behind the mug.

"He was curious about when I'd last heard from you." There was accusation in her voice that implied Nicole's duties as a daughter were lacking. "I told him you were a busy woman but we'd talked about a month ago. I had no idea you'd gone on a cruise. To the Mediterranean on an Italian line, no less. Linus has always been so stanchly American. Why would he choose a foreign ship?"

"He wished to be anonymous," Nicole said. Her gaze focused on the artificial centerpiece made up of tall, willowy white flowers, her thoughts far away.

"Well that went bad. The ship sank for pity's sake. How can a famous man be anonymous on a ship that sinks?"

Austin tuned out Mercedes's diatribe as he considered what the call had meant. The head of Black Adder needed to find out if Nicole might come here and gambled she wouldn't. As late as yesterday Austin would have agreed with him.

"Where did you find calla lilies at this time of year?"

Austin gave the centerpiece another look.

"A florist in Denver orders them. They're pretty, aren't they? He sent me an email saying he was expecting hydrangeas next week and I should come by."

This woman had way too much time on her hands if she drove to Denver for out-of-season flowers in January. But he also realized if the conversation had come down to centerpieces, the mother and daughter needed privacy to talk without his presence. "I'd like to wash my hands. May I use your restroom?"

Mercedes pointed to a doorway. "Down the hall. Third door on the left."

Austin stepped into the hall and out of sight, then leaned against the wall to listen. He only had to wait a moment before Mercedes spoke. "I gather you've left the Senator. You finally get your life on track and settle on someone worthwhile, then throw it all away."

Her tone was stressed. It was small wonder the women weren't close. Mercedes hadn't asked about why or how Nicole escaped or about her grandchild. And he noted with interest, Nicole hadn't volunteered any information.

"Linus is a sadistic bastard. If I stayed with him it was only a matter of time before he killed me."

Austin was impressed. Nicole rarely painted the world in such black and white tones.

"You never forgive and always had such a flair for exaggeration."

He imagined the shaking of her mother's head that accompanied her tone.

"Never forgive? What are you talking about?" Nicole raised her voice. A full-blown argument was under way.

"This is just like that incident with your

father. You never forgave him."

Even Austin was shocked by Mercedes's accusation.

"I never forgave him?" Nicole was practically sputtering. "You immediately remarried Brad and systematically erased him from our lives."

"Yes, but eventually I forgave him."

"Was this before or after he got his own daughter pregnant?" Nicole's voice betrayed her hurt and Austin wanted to go to her, but didn't. She and her mother had to work this out.

"He said Beth was pregnant when she came to him and he even offered to pay for an abortion."

Austin had dealt with enough sinners to know everything could be justified – even incest.

"You believed him?"

"Of course, I never doubted his veracity."

A loud snort followed that statement which he assumed was from Nicole. "Except when he lied about molesting children."

"He never lied. That was his downfall."

Her words would have been a punch in the gut to Nicole. He could well imagine her shock and hurt.

"You. Knew. Before. He. Was. Arrested?"

Oh, man. His family was screwed up, but her family was just as bad.

"Don't use that tone with me. You've obviously learned nothing. Marriage is not perfect. Sometimes you have to turn a blind eye to your husband imperfections."

"Imperfections? He went to jail for having sex with young girls – not one, several."

"That was all overblown. The sex was consensual. Those girls weren't that young."

"Mother! Sex with a ten-year-old is never consensual."

"You're making too big a deal of this. That happened over twenty years ago. He's a changed man and so am I. I've learned to forgive like you should do with Linus. Go home. Tell him you love him. That man could be President of the United States one day. Think of it. You could live in the White House."

Austin wondered if there was something in the water that made mothers delusional. His own mother lived in fear of her ex-husband, but dated the same type of bully over and over. And could never understand why her sons hated them all. Until Rod Stevens quietly stepped in and took over their lives. He was the one man who had their best interest at heart.

"I don't love Linus and never have," Nicole said. He heard the scraping of a chair and knew someone was standing. "He will never be President and I only married him to protect

Libby."

"You shouldn't have gotten involved. The state would have taken that child."

"And institutionalized her."

"Which happened anyway. She's better off where she was."

"No, she wasn't. She deserves to have a loving family around her. Her life has been hard enough without being put away."

"Drama. Drama. Drama. I hope you're not thinking of taking up with this man you've brought home. He's handsome, I'll grant you. But he'll never be able to support you like the Senator can."

Austin held his breath. Mercedes may have been wrong about a lot of things, but she was right about this.

"I love him."

His heart leapt into his throat.

"You're a fool. Look at him. He's nothing but a muscle-bound pretty boy. Linus has an air about him. When he walks into a room, people notice."

The silence made him uncomfortable. Had her mother worn her down enough that Nicole thought she made sense?

"True."

*No. Please don't think that.* Beads of sweat broke out on his forehead.

"Linus and many of his friends have the John Wayne swagger. Everybody acts so tough these days. Arrogance and belligerence have been elevated to an art form."

His sigh of relief told him he'd been holding his breath waiting for her answer.

"Austin doesn't have any of that."

*Was that a good thing or a bad?*

"He's the toughest man I've ever met, and yet he's unfailing polite and gentle. People are rarely what they seem. Funny, I should have learned that lesson a long time ago."

"Listen to me." Mercedes had been reduced to begging. "You are infatuated, but you will regret this."

Austin closed his eyes. He feared exactly the same thing.

"We have to go. Please don't tell anybody you've seen me. I don't want Linus to hear I'm alive from anybody but me. He deserves that at the very least."

"Go? No, stay. You'll be safe here. I'll call the salon and get you an appointment. Your hair can be fixed, then you'll be back to being pretty again. You'll feel better and see I'm right."

A silence fell. Austin pushed off the wall and started toward the kitchen when Nicole spoke again. "I've sent you a bunch of paperwork that Gerry agreed to save over the years. What happened to it?"

Austin's footsteps halted as surely as if he were a vehicle at a red light. He'd spent hours wondering how anyone could be around Nicole without realizing how smart she was. But this was how she did it. The best description he could come up with was Columbo's exit style. "Just one last thing." That thing, of course, would be the zinger.

"It's in the safe. Shall I get it?"

"If it's convenient."

Interesting. She appeared disinterested, but he bet whatever was in the safe she was desperate to have. A bunch of paperwork could turn out to be any number of things.

He waited in the foyer, trying not to look eager to leave. So far nothing about her mother had impressed him. No wonder Nicole's life had been so screwed up. Bad parenting always meant messed up kids. Look at him and his brothers.

"Is this it?" Mercedes asked. The office was located on the far side of the living room.

"Wow. There's a lot of it, isn't there?"

*Did she need his help?*

"Sit here. We'll go through it and you can discard what you no longer need."

"I can't. We've got to go. I'll sort it in the car."

"You're determined to leave the Senator?"

"Yes."

"Mark my words, the man you brought here will not provide you with the security that Linus would. This will be a huge mistake."

"Mother, all my life I've followed your advice. I'm afraid if I continue to do so, I will get is what I've always gotten – grief, fear, and heartache. I refused to live like that anymore. I have to make my own decisions. And the one thing I know is that if I'm ever to have happiness, my only chance is with Austin."

"Nobody's life is perfect. I've done the best job I could for you."

"I know, but it's time for me to find my own path."

He met her in the hallway and escorted her silently out the door and into the waiting car. Nicole and her mother air-kissed one more time. Neither spoke of the future.

Settling behind the wheel, he put the car in drive and slowly left the grounds unable to recall a time when his life was filled with such promise, but good things rarely lasted. In the past when a woman got serious, he'd panic. This time was different.

She loved him, and he wasn't running for safety. Maybe tomorrow things would be different when she got a hard look at his lifestyle, but for today things were good. He drove to a public rest area on the highway, he'd seen earlier.

"Drive to Portland or fly?" he asked as Nicole shuffled though the paperwork that lay in piles on the seat, the floor board and her lap.

She raised her head at his question. "Portland?" Then shook her head. "No. If I am ever going to be free I have to face my husband. Lake Forest."

Briefly a scene flashed before his eyes of their confrontation. She truly had no idea how ruthless her husband could be. The Senator wouldn't be alone. His bodyguards would be there. All armed. Except one – Tyrone. It might be a blood bath, but they had a fighting chance. He wanted to refuse. To tell her it wasn't safe. But sometimes one had to face his devils to be free.

*He had broken into the house through a rear window being careful to wear gloves and not track dirt. The place had been trashed. Empty liquor bottles, overflowing ash trays, cockroaches, dishes piled in the sink. The house hadn't looked like this when his mother had lived there.*

*His father's gun was loaded in the nightstand. How many times had he reached for it in a fight? How many times had he pointed it at his sons? His wife? One night he shot the dog, an old mutt named Scout. They'd packed the next day and left before he returned from work, each positive the next bullet wouldn't be a miss.*

*The internet had been his coach. He knew about the safety and how to cock the pistol. He waited, watching the minutes tick by on the alarm clock by the bed. The kitchen clock struck midnight. He counted each chime. Soon. Seventeen minutes later the pickup rumpled to a stop in the driveway. How many nights had that sound terrorized him? The drape covered him, but he held his breath from the stench of old cigarette smoke and household dust.*

*The front door banged open. The crash that followed echoed through the rooms of the small house. The monster who called himself his father, stumbled into the bedroom and flung himself face down on the bed, mumbling unintelligible words. Then silence. Several minutes later a loud snore. Austin counted to twenty-five, slid out from his hiding place and fired six shots into the body on the bed. At the seventh squeeze of the trigger, the gun clicked.*

*No more bullets. Quietly he laid the gun on the bed. No one would believe six shots in the back was suicide. He left through the front door. Once outside the house he listed for sirens, but heard none. Apparently the sound of gunshots weren't unusual enough to merit calling the police.*

He understood Nicole had to do this. A woman who declared she wanted to walk in the sunshine had to be free in her heart. If it came to gun-play, how would she feel if he was the one who took her husband down?

The first thing he had to do was call Travis.

His brother could out-strategize anyone even a naïve wife walking into a lion's den. He glanced at the woman sitting next to him. She wasn't a fool. She was the bravest woman he'd ever met and smart. Surely between Nicole and Travis they could defeat the Senator with something other than bullets.

Nicole's attention had returned to the paperwork as Austin grabbed his sat phone and stepped out of the car.

# Chapter Twenty-One

There was very little one could say about the flat landscape of Nebraska except there was a lot of it, over five hundred miles of endless highway intersected farmers' fallow fields from Fort Collins to Omaha. Mozart had been raised in Nebraska. Austin could understand his eagerness to leave. The weather provided the only diversion. Snow preceded freezing rain to be followed by more snow all under a gloomy overcast sky.

Neither reached for the radio and for the longest time the only noise in the car was the sound of the windshield wipers repetitive clicking and Nicole opening brown envelopes and flipping pages.

When the endless snow covered cornfields bored him beyond reason, Austin finally broke the silence. "What is all that?"

She glanced up, pausing for a moment. "Among other things, it is my pre-nup, but it is also a bunch of paperwork I signed over the years. What do you know about political Super Pacs?"

He shook his head. "Nothing."

"Me, either, but Linus was forever having

me sign paperwork, apparently related to a
Super Pac called National Pride."

"Why you?"

"Apparently it is an LLC and I am the
President which I never knew. He'd open up a
document, point to a line for my signature, insist
I use my maiden name, then snatch it way and
pop it in the safe. Early on I asked what I was
signing only to be fed some poorly fabricated lie,
but after a while he didn't even bother to do
that. So at night after the house was quiet I'd
slip downstairs, open the safe, copy the
documents, then send the packet to my mother
for storage figuring if he was being sneaky, there
was a reason why."

"Linus didn't trust you but he gave you the
combination to the safe?"

She chuckled, but the she wasn't amused.
"Good heavens, no. I figured it out."

Austin gave her a sideways glance only to
see her attention was on the documents in front
of her.

"One of Linus' favorite stories," she
continued absently, "Is of his father trusting him
with the safe combination. He was six. Nobody
else in the entire world has ever known the
combination but father and son. In his mind it
was a huge honor. The combination had to be
something easy enough for a six year old to

remember." Her tone was distracted. She was silent for several minutes while she read.

"Like a birthdate or an address?" He finally forced himself to ask to get her attention again. She looked up at the sound of his words.

"Exactly. It took me all of three tries to figure it out. When he announced the cruise, I knew it was the first opportunity I had to leave. Living with Linus was a prison. I was never alone. A guard was always with me, so I couldn't shop or meet a friend for lunch or do anything normal."

She'd been prepared with an IBS and a dry suit when she'd gotten on the boat. Somehow she'd gotten around the shopping issue.

"Linus speaks out of both sides of his mouth. What he wants and what he says are two very different things. When we were first together he used to talk about our having children."

Austin's stomach roiled. "You were planning to get pregnant?"

"Not in this lifetime. Nor did he want a child, but he couldn't resist dangling the carrot. So I insisted we prepare a nursery. I spent months and thousands of dollars renovating one of the third floor rooms into a nursery, knowing the entire time he'd had a vasectomy. But he also could never object to any purchase. I bought a wide assortment of things, I spent months ordering random items and then returning them, so that he never knew how much money I spent or what I kept. In the end, I'd acquired everything I thought I needed to leave a cruise ship."

That gave him pause. She'd entered the marriage knowing it wouldn't last and both partners were both using each other. She was a beautiful woman and he admired her, but it was obvious that they had different ideas of what a marriage entailed.

For the first time it occurred to him that she might not meet his requirements for a wife. Was she only pretending to like him so he'd take care of her? Was she already planning to leave? Never had he ever felt this way about a woman. But even so he'd been careful not to reveal his feelings.

He mulled that information over in his mind as the miles rolled by, trying to sort his feelings. How could he have been so crazy about her only to be incredibly disappointed?

The back of his neck tingled. Nicole's gaze was pinned to his face. "What?" he asked.

"You tell me. Waves of anger are radiating off you. Obviously, I said something to piss you off."

He didn't want to discuss this. He hadn't decided how he felt or what words to use to let her down easily. But it didn't matter. This was a topic to discuss after her safety was no longer in question.

"What is your plan for dealing with the Senator?"

She laughed. "I thought you called this my game? Change the topic to avoid the question?"

"I wasn't changing the topic," he lied. He glanced at her arched eyebrow. "Okay, maybe I was, but we can't talk about this now."

"We can't discuss why you are angry?"

"I'm not angry."

She loudly sighed. "Let me run back the tape and figure out what ticked you off. Linus? Birth control? Vasectomy? Lying? You're angry that I knew I couldn't get pregnant and yet made a production number of decoration a nursery?"

"No. That was a clever diversion. Tell me how you met Linus."

"Oh, that story. Let me warn you it's not my proudest moment. To justify it I could say I was desperate, but hindsight as made me realize financial ruin would have been a better alternative." She stared out the window.

"Beth's accident was in early summer." Her voice was far removed as though she had a traveled back in time. "My insurance refused to cover Libby due to legal complications, pre-existing conditions, and the usual BS they send out. Her medical bills were skyrocketing. Within weeks I stared at invoices demanding over one hundred and fifty thousand dollars. She needed constant care. I kept cutting my hours at work until the library laid me off. Four house payments behind with bankruptcy staring me in the face, I had to do something."

She turned her head and read his body language before continuing. Austin held steady not moving, but she was sharp. His white-knuckle death grip on the wheel would hardly go unnoticed.

"A friend of mine in Chicago worked for a local congressman who'd just lost his wife. She urged me to visit. So I spent my last bit of money on a new hair style, a fabulous dress, and an airplane ticket to attend a fund-raising dinner. I wasn't the Congressman's type, but Linus was in attendance and he latched onto me – squiring me around the room, introducing me to friends and colleagues like I was his date. We sat together during the meal. I felt pretty and carefree for the first time since the accident. He flirted and I encouraged him. But like with all Cinderella stories, the clock struck midnight. He wanted more, but my pride wouldn't let me go through with it."

She made a self-depreciated sound. "In fact I told him I would be the worst thing in the world for him. I had debts up the wazoo and cared for a brain-damaged child. He backed away as any intelligent man would have. I was desperate but even in the beginning I could tell he wanted me to be someone I wasn't."

"So what happened?"

"I flew home." Her voice was casual, but her shoulders were rigid and a small line appeared between her eyebrows.

"Do you want some ibuprofen?"

"No." As she smiled, he found his heart lightened.

"So you flew home…"

"Three days later, he showed up on my door step and convinced me to marry him. By the time I learned about the vasectomy and had a better handle on the man himself, he'd already paid or negotiated away my debts. But it wasn't until he produced the pre-nup that I knew I couldn't do it."

"The document didn't endow you with all his worldly possessions?"

"Originally it stated that I was entitled to a hundred-thousand-dollars for each year we were together, minus expenses and any gifts or jewelry would be returned to the estate including my wedding ring."

Austin hid his shock, not that Linus was a self-serving smuck, but that he'd gone so far as to put it in writing. "So before the marriage had even begun you owed him money? Did you sign it?"

"Of course not. I gave him back his ring and said 'thank you very much'. But Linus understands indebtedness better than anyone I'd ever known. He settled my mortgage debt by purchasing the loan. So no matter what, I owed him. In the process of being saved, I'd lost my home. Rather than argue, I packed. Every morning his lawyer showed up with newly revised pre-nup. Each morning I read it then refused to sign, all the while the lawyer assuring me this was the best offer I was going to get. All it involved was selling my soul."

Austin kept his face expressionless. "So how did he finally win?"

She sighed. "He wooed my mother to his cause. I'm not saying this to justify my action, but I was so alone and so lonely. Libby is wonderful, but wearing. I caved."

No wonder she rarely spoke to her family. He stared at her, only glancing occasionally at the flat highway as the car sped alone. "I investigated you before I met you. Everything about you screamed Disney Princess. Being a wealthy senator's wife is the dream of a lot of women I've known. It was only after I met you that I realized your life is as far from perfect as it gets."

She paused, staring out the window at the snow covered ground. "He loved his first wife. She passed out in the bathtub from a combination of drugs and alcohol and drowned. Men don't change who they innately are. Even loving her, he must have been cruel. The facts were down-played, but I believe she killed herself."

"And his second wife?"

"Rumor was she was having an affair with a colleague of his. I'm confident he had Gunter drown in the pool, but even if that wasn't true, he certainly didn't miss her."

"But I still don't understand. Layton doesn't strike me as an impulsive guy. Why was he so determined to marry you?"

A sad smile curled her lips. "To him I fit the image of a successful man's wife. It's why he insisted that I was always dressed to the nines. In three years of marriage not one day was casual Friday."

"Did you choose drowning as a cause of death to put the finger of blame on him?"

"I told you this wasn't my finest hour." Her lips tightened. "If I went missing and wasn't found while on a cruise. It would look like I fallen overboard – or had been pushed. With two previous wives dead by drowning, I wanted to taint him with enough suspicion that even though they couldn't prove he'd caused my death, his political life would be ruined."

# Chapter Twenty-Two

*Evanston, Illinois*
*Monday, January 23rd*

Travis Stevens parked the rented van on the narrow winding street in front of the quaint B&B about thirty minutes south of Lake Forest. As he inched his way between parked cars, he scanned the windows of the stone mini-castle complete with two turrets separated by a long balcony with a stone wall.

One look at the B&B and he was doubly glad Abigail had chosen not to join him. This place was right out of 'Romeo and Juliet' and went against everything in his basic SEAL training. He could imagine Abby plotting a re-enactment, and while he didn't mind scaling the wall, he hated reciting poetry or in this case flowery Shakespearean tongue-twisting words.

Nicole Layton must have his brother tied up in knots if he agreed to stay here. The thought amused him. No woman had ever laid claim to Austin. High time someone did.

The door opened before he could get his hand in the air to knock. The canopied bed took up the bulk of the circular bedroom. Travis restrained a groan. "Where's Nicole?"

"Hairdresser." The manner in which his brother spit out the word spoke volumes about whose decision it had been.

Travis had long come to understand that a man understood hierarchy and might follow your leadership based on rank alone, but he'd never met a woman who hadn't made him peddle three times harder to be the one in charge.

To needle Austin, he asked, "You let her go alone?"

Austin glanced at this watch. "No. She. Went. Alone. I had an entirely different plan."

Travis suppressed his grin. "I thought she was the timid type."

"Timid? No." He snorted. "She has no problem going after what she wants." He glanced at his watch a second time. "How long does a damn appointment take?"

Travis rubbed his chin and pondered the question. "How long has she been gone?"

"Almost an hour." Austin paced to the glass balcony doors and studied the street.

"Only an hour? You might as well sit down. It usually takes Abby half a day."

"You're kidding?"

Travis shook his head and Austin begrudgingly came back to the small table, tossed the ruffled cushion to the ground and sat gingerly on the edge of the dainty chair.

Travis wasn't prepared to risk it and he chose the bed as a steadier alternative. "Let's go over the plan while we've got time."

Austin's head bobbed, indicating he'd heard the words but his fingers drummed the table and he twitched in his seat.

He had it bad. "Have you told her you love her?" Travis asked.

Austin hopped up from his chair and stormed to the glass door again. "I don't know how I feel about her. When she talks about being together, it includes the child. You know how we were raised. What kind of father would I make?"

"You are nothing like our father. He was a sadistic drug addict." Travis spied the mini-bar disguised as part of the armoire and opened the refrigerator. Despite the early morning hour, he grabbed two beers, twisted the caps and thrust one at Austin.

"I've always meant to tell you this."

Something about his tone had Travis's full attention. Austin gripped the neck of the bottle and stared at the label.

"I don't know why I haven't." He crossed the room, sank into the chair and ran a hand through his hair. "I killed him."

Travis shoved his beer onto table and knelt

beside his brother and wrapped his arms around Austin. "I know. I knew as soon as I heard he was dead that you'd done it. People have always thought I was the one in charge, but even as a child you always had a core of toughness I envied."

Austin pushed away. "You knew? You never said anything."

"I figured you hadn't told me for a reason."

"Oh, God. I've carried around this secret for years and you already knew." Austin barked out a shaky laugh and rose to pace to the windows and back.

The cold beer slid down Travis's throat as he thought about what to say. "Did you realize that you stopped stuttering the day he died?"

"I did?" He spoke to the window, and then turned. "Well, you'll be glad to know that I've taken it back up with Nicole."

Travis remembered that kicked in the gut feeling he had when he realized Abby was the one. "Does she know about Dad?"

He grimaced. "Yeah, she claims it was justified because I was defending the family."

Travis couldn't help but like a woman who saw his brother as he truly was. "She's right. How does she feel about you?"

Austin crossed the room, but this time he sat on the bed next to his brother. "She's talking marriage." He dropped his head to his hands.

"And you haven't told her you love her? She's a brave woman." Travis refused to take another swallow of beer for fear he'd choke on his laughter. Fortunately, his brother didn't notice.

"At first I thought she was so unattainable, but as I've come to realize that she has had to fight as hard as we did to leave the ugliness behind."

Travis threw his arm companionably around his brother's shoulders. "And she's still doing it. How do you feel about her seeing the Senator?"

"Proud. Scared. I want to hide her away and protect her, but she wants to be free. 'To walk in the sun' is how she expresses it. The one thing our father's death taught me was that one can only get there if they face down their demons. But if I have to kill her husband, I don't know if our relationship will survive."

"It will. You love her. Loving a woman changes a man. But know now I'm going to be damn angry dancing at your wedding before my own." Travis was glad to see Austin chuckle.

"Abby will come around. She loves you."

Travis eyed the French doors that opened onto the balcony. "Maybe I should have brought her and done the 'Romeo, Romeo, wherefore art thou?' thing on the balcony."

"Dude, that's not your line. That's hers."

A loud knock had Austin jumping from the bed and flinging open the door. His brother Sam grinned, took one look around the fussy room and gave a low whistle.

"I wasn't expecting you."

"I wasn't expecting this." He gestured with a sweep of his hand. The brothers hugged, and Sam slapped him on the back.

"Why are you here?"

"When you're in deep dodo has The Cube ever let you down? I could smell the stench in Portland so I decided to drop by. Lend a hand. That sort of thing. On the way I picked up an old friend." He stepped aside. Zack Pritchard stood behind.

Austin gaped. How long had it been? Five years? "What are you doing here?"

"Thought you might need a driver." Zack took a look around the room. "But it looks like you need some decorating advice. Let's get out of here before I get in touch with my feminine side – something Chloe claims I never do."

"How is she?" Travis and Austin asked together.

Zack grinned, gesturing with a hand to indicate her size. "Pregnant."

Travis thumped his friend on the back. "Congratulations! I can't believe you left her at home."

"She insisted."

Sam hooted. "Actually, she aimed a gun at him and demanded he leave so she and the 'baby SEAL' could get some room to breathe." As he spoke he raised his finger to indicate quotation marks around the words baby SEAL.

Austin handed a beer to Zack and a bottle of water to Sam. "A boy. You're having a boy."

Travis heard the undertone in his voice. Yep, if he was even thinking about children, Nicole was the one.

"Chloe thinks I'm hovering."

Travis groaned. "Yeah, Abby has a few choice words to say about my hyper-possessive behavior. Speaking of Abby… "

The Donna Karan was on sale. It was sleek, black, and showed enough curves, cleavage and leg that she radiated sex appeal in a way she'd avoided for the past three years. The mud brown hair was gone and longer, thanks to extensions. A multitude of interwoven warm colors highlighted her face. Her makeup had been professionally applied. She looked good. And best of all, she'd paid for all it with Linus's cash he'd left in the safe in his money belt.

Parking was tight at the B&B, so she found a side street space for the rental car. Wanting

Austin's reaction to her new look, she left everything in the car and strolled around the corner. The quiet B&B had men swarming all over it. Two men on the balcony held a rope. Halfway up the rope a third man slowly scaled the stone wall, reciting a brutalized version of Shakespeare at the top of his lungs. Through it all Austin was holding a cell phone, filming it.

She stopped walking, trying to piece together what was happening.

"Holy cow," One of men holding the rope said as he released it and stared open mouthed. The man halfway up the wall dropped into the bushes, yelling, "Hey."

The third man laughed. Austin lost focus on filming the scene. His stunned look was worth every penny of the seven thousand dollars she'd spent.

"I saw her first," rope guy yelled, but it was too late.

Austin leapt over the wall and landed on the lawn. "The hell you did." He grinned.

She held out her arms and pivoted for his approval.

"Oh, baby. You look…"

"Beautiful."

"Breath-taking."

"Hot."

The three men offered suggestions in loud,

obvious whispers. Nicole laughed as Austin came closer as if he was afraid to touch her. He clasped her hand and held her at arm's length while his gaze roamed her body.

"You remember…" He gestured behind him in a vague way.

"Travis, his brother." The Shakespearean actor dry tone conveyed his disgust as he brushed the dirt off his pants.

Two other thumps followed. All the men were on the ground and being introduced. Nicole looked from one man to the other. "What were you doing?"

The men guffawed. Sam slapped Travis on the back. "You tell her."

"Um… trying to get my girlfriend to marry me."

"She likes Romeo and Juliet?"

"She's a girl. She's a writer. What's not to love?"

"Well, for one thing the play was a tragedy. Not a romance."

He shrugged. "Probably not my best strategy, but I've tried everything else so it was worth a shot."

# Chapter Twenty-Three

*Tuesday, January 24th*
*Lake Forest, Illinois*

The wooded area on the side of the Layton estate made the perfect place for the team to coordinate. The paneled rental van wedged between the trees blended with snow-covered ground. The four men she'd met earlier had transformed into a military fighting unit each wearing tactical suits of full body armor, combat boots, and about nine hundred pounds of gear, stashed in pockets, on belts and strapped to their leg. Nicole didn't understand how they are even able to walk. Yet each man seemed perfectly comfortable with his load. She could see the adrenaline surge in the set of their mouths, jaws and shoulders while hers manufactured itself in nervous flutters.

A folding table held a set of floor plans. Sam operated a heat sensor hooked up to a computer monitor. She didn't ask where they'd gotten the equipment she was still puzzled by who had arrived to help. When she decided to confront her husband, her thought had been a one-on-one conversation with Austin waiting in the car.

But the one thing she'd learned was that the

Stevens brothers operated with a plan. Other than, "Hello, Linus" she hadn't figured out what words to use if he survived her greeting without having a heart attack.

Sam curled his fingers for Nicole to come closer, which was easier said than done. She'd donned closed-toed flats, but the snow drifts came over the top. Her stocking feet were icy cold and wet. Austin's jacket covered her to mid-thigh and he'd given her a scarf for her neck and a pair of socks to cover her hands.

The intense atmosphere made her nervous. The tactical suits upped the game. She touched Sam's vest, longing to open each pocket and examine the contents. "You are dressed for war."

"And you aren't?" He referred to her make over.

It was true, but she'd envisioned the battlefield on a different level. Certainly without weapons.

"How many people will be in the house?" Sam asked.

Nicole had lost track of time. "What day is it?"

"Tuesday."

*Had it really been only eleven days since she'd jumped overboard? And she'd thought she'd been clever with all her preparation. Looking at these men prepare, convinced her that most of her success had been beginner's luck.*

"On Tuesday the cleaning team comes at ten and is usually gone by one. What time is it now?"

"Two-thirty."

"The cook will be fixing dinner. There will be a security guard at the front gate, one or two either in the house or walking around outside, but usually they hang out in the kitchen. Linus will be in his office on the second floor. He likes Gunter close, so he will be in the same room or just outside the door."

Sam listened, studying the floor plans as she spoke. The men were each unique, but with obvious differences. Zack appeared the most easy-going, but she suspected that was because he'd been away from the military the longest. He'd entertained them with stories of life in the fast lane at Indianapolis, but it wasn't until he talked about his wife that she could see he had the same possessive streak as both Austin and Travis and how much he openly adored Chloe.

Sam stood out from the group. Even if she hadn't known he was a police officer, his posture and interrogation skills clued her into his profession. While the other men chatted, Sam grilled her on details.

The two of them leaned over the plans as she pointed to the various rooms that would be in use. While he didn't say anything she sensed a frustration her answers hadn't solved. "What?"

He straightened, looking her in the eyes. "Listen. It's none of my business, but if this guard, Gunter, spent as much time in your husband's presence as you indicate, he would have known you were being abused."

Heat crept up her cheeks. Her first instinct was to lie, but Sam's expression was concern, not censure. She'd never told anyone the truth. Austin hadn't asked, but as she glanced around, she realized each of the men had stopped their tasks and listened for her answer.

Swallowing was difficult. Austin made a move toward her, but Sam flicked his hand palm out to stop him.

"Breathe," Austin said in a low voice.

Nicole drew in a long breath and exhaled completely.

Sam's gaze never left her face. "Good," he encouraged her with a soothing tone.

This man risked his life for hers. He didn't know her. At the very least he was entitled to the truth. All of these men deserved to know what her husband was really like.

Her voice came out in a whisper. "He knew."

Sam's mouth tightened. "Was he in the room at any time when it happened?"

"He was the one who held my hands behind

my back." Her teeth chattered as she remembered how Gunter would block the door so she couldn't escape. His eyes flat. His body aroused.

Linus loved inflicting pain, but it turned Gunter on. She shuddered. Her stomach seized.

Austin sprinted across the ground to reach her. "She's freezing. I'm going to get her to the car." One of his muscular arms came around her waist.

"No. She needs to be here. Find something for her to stand on so her feet are out of the snow," Sam said.

Travis handed over a wooden crate and helped Nicole balance. Zack found a thin solar blanket to wrap around her shoes and ankles to warm her.

"Look at the screen," Sam instructed. "Every place you see the infra red is a human. Nobody's on the third floor."

She nodded as the others crowded around. Zack placed his hand on her shoulder to help ground her.

"The nursery," she said quietly. The men were silent. She realized her mistake. "It's not what you think. The nursery was my sanctuary to get away from everyone and be alone for a few hours."

Sam tapped the floor plan. "Travis, this is

your insertion place."

Nicole pointed to a dormer window. "This window isn't locked. Walk on left edge of the stairs as you go down to avoid the sound carrying throughout the house."

The men listened intently, nodding as she spoke.

"Tyrone will join Zack to neutralize the guards on the perimeter and in the kitchen after he's opened the gate for you and the press," Sam said.

Nicole almost fell off the box. "The press?" Austin's arm steadied her. She directed her question to him. "Why is the press coming? I don't want this known."

"Yes, you do. Layton will never honor an agreement between you if he can figure a way around it."

"Making a public announcement will ruin him. What would keep him from coming after me then?"

"We are playing this by ear, but if you think you're safe then make your announcement only about the divorce. Remember you'll be in the room alone with Layton, but I'll be nearby."

"Nicole," Travis said. "Don't underestimate him. He'll be desperate. He's probably already got wind of the FBI investigation. Fox News ran an item on the deaths of his first two wives early this morning leaving some open questions about how three women married to the same man could drown. Conservatives are his base, he's got to be worried."

Zack handed her a small flesh colored ear piece. "Wear this ear bud so we can hear everything that is being said. You'll be able to hear us, too. We're your backup, but we won't interfere unless you need us. Remember you hold the upper hand, but he has nothing to lose, so be careful. Keep yourself safe at all costs."

Austin's phone dinged. He read the text message. "Good news. Elena and Libby are in hiding. So your husband can't use them as a threat."

"Can you get them on the next plane?" Travis asked.

"No. Libby's not doing well. Hooch's hiding place is a hospital. As soon as he can get them on a plane, he will." He winked at Nicole. "Are we ready?"

Nicole leaned into him to gather his strength to her. Trees sheltered the group from being seen, but a flat span of snow-covered grass separated them from the house. "How are we getting there?"

"You're driving to the front door. Our man at the gate will let you in. I'll be in the back seat. Once inside the gate drive slowly to give everyone time to get in place."

# Chapter Twenty Four

The former SEALs made it sound so easy and to them it probably was. Certainly driving to the door was less painful than rowing all night. Her stress level had surpassed orange and was deep into red. Fear had been a motivating factor when she jumped off the ship, but she'd been operating on automatic pilot. Her life had been the only one in jeopardy. Now she was responsible for four men in addition. Her nerves were sending distress signals to radio towers underneath her skin.

She inhaled, working to calm herself the way Austin had taught her. In the backseat under a blanket he hunkered down. A large unknown black man operated the gate.

"Welcome home, Mrs. Layton."

She glanced in the rear view mirror to see if anyone was behind her. But when her gaze returned to the guard station, the man was gone.

"Was that Tyrone?" she raised her voice to ask Austin. It startled her when he answered quietly in the affirmative in her ear.

The gate remained open. Linus would throw a fit. She almost stopped the car to close it. After all this time, she still worried about her husband's reaction. No more.

"Are you okay back there?" she asked needing to hear the reassuring sound of his voice.

"I'm fine. You're doing great. Don't worry about me."

She parked in the place he'd indicated, climbed out of the car, tossing the jacket across the front seat and slid her feet into the fabulous Jimmie Choos. Immediately the chill in the air hit her. She unlatched the rear door and left it slightly ajar as she headed for the front steps.

The entrance hall was empty. The sterile white-on-white décor screamed of the emptiness of the lives of those who lived here.

No one greeted her. No one stopped her. Despite the noise of her heels echoing on the marble foyer she was invisible. She took a deep breath, grabbed the handrail and marched up the sweeping curved staircase, conscious of every noise.

In her ear she heard Travis's tranquil voice asking quietly. "Everyone in place?" Murmured voices affirmed. "Nicole, you're good to go."

The hallway mirror allowed her to check her appearance. A little pale, perhaps. She pinched her cheeks to heighten her color and strode the length of the corridor. For once her mother had been right. She felt better when she looked good.

In the past she would have knocked before entering Linus's private study, but today she grasped the handle, heard Austin's quiet words of encouragement, grasped the handle and turned it.

"Hello, Linus." Careful not to close the door completely, she set her purse containing the video camera on the table, the way she'd been instructed.

Linus, much to her disappointment, did not have a heart attack. And she was even sorrier to say that his look of surprise lasted less long than she hoped. Gunter, on the other hand backed against the window frame, his outstretched arm attempted to ward her presence off.

"Hello, my dear." With an expression of grim determination, Linus rose from his chair. His eyes glinted in a way she'd usually saw before he beat her.

Momentary fear held her rigid.

Then she inhaled and calmed. She refused to be controlled by fear. Her body didn't even struggle when she looked at her husband with nothing but distain in her eyes.

"You've made it home." As usual his expression conveyed his disappointment with her actions. "What a pity. I've wasted a great deal of money hunting for you."

Gunter recovered enough to lower his arm

and revert to his usual glare. Nicole focused on her husband, confident the security guard would do nothing without his boss's command. "You once told me there was no amount of money you wouldn't spend to have me by your side."

With raised eyebrows a small smile played around his lips. "Those words have turned out to be quite prophetic."

She worked to maintain her cool stance. Her confidence surged when his gaze traveled the length of her body and lust reflected in his eyes.

"I've dropped by to inform you I'm filing for divorce."

"Divorce?" A harsh bark. His eyes flashed. Linus sneered. "You're already dead. A dead person can't get a divorce."

"But as you see I'm standing here in front of you, alive, alert, and capable of hiring an attorney. So I doubt if the courts will see it your way."

Linus stepped from behind the desk, stalking toward her. Her instinct was to move backward, but she clung to her ground.

"I see. So what is it that you want?" His voice was oily smooth.

She hated him. "Nothing that wasn't agreed to in the pre-nup. I'll keep your secrets. You'll marry again. Any controversy will blow over."

He stood close enough to strike her, but

Nicole no longer feared his physical threats. He might get a blow in, but Austin wouldn't let him get two.

"The pre-nup?" Linus laughed. His hand ran up her arm in a caress.

A voice screamed in her head. That was what he heard? The part about money? She'd misjudged the situation thinking his reputation meant more to him than money.

Still stroking her arm, he leaned closer and spoke in a low voice. "I think you'll be surprised at the changes that have been made to our little agreement since our happy union took place."

She jerked her arm away and stepped out of his reach. "I have an original."

He was content to let her go and leaned back to rest against the edge of the desk, studying his fingernails. "My dear, you are entitled to nothing. I have no intention of allowing you to interfere with my plans. Granted it would have been easier to have a dutiful wife by my side, but the public loves a grieving widower. I've played that role before."

He flicked his fingers toward Gunter. A slow smile crossed the guard's face as he pushed off from the wall.

"I know about the Super Pac, National Pride." She whirled on her husband and spoke quickly. "If I die, it goes public."

The Senator held up his hand to halt Gunter's action without looking in his direction. Out of the corner of her eye, Nicole saw movement, but while the bodyguard may have been the one with the muscle, the most dangerous person in the room was her husband. No matter what the other man was doing her focus was narrowed to Linus.

"My, my. You have been busy, haven't you? How do you plan to make it public?" He tilted his head when he spoke to convey curiosity rather than a perceived threat.

No wonder she'd lost every argument with him. "I have copies of everything I've signed."

His eyes narrowed. Two angry red spots appeared in his cheeks. "You've had the combination to the safe for a while, haven't you? Truly, I do believe I underestimated you. However, you're bluffing. You have no friends. There is no one who will make this public. And if you are thinking of your mother, she'll burn the documents herself if I offer her husband an ambassadorship."

He laughed. Austin had been correct. He would never honor any agreement. Her life was forfeit. Linus knew he'd won, she could see it in his expression. She wanted to yell for the other men to help, but her husband would kill them as easily as he would her.

"Now you can shoot her." He spoke without turning around.

Even knowing what he was, the casualness of the command still shocked her. His evil grin told her of his pleasure in seeing her die. She braced herself.

When the room was silent, she forced herself to turn her attention to the windows. Where had Gunter gone?

"Gunter?" Linus asked, turning at the same time. A balcony door stood ajar and the sheer drape fluttered. "Gunter!" He stormed to the opening to check the balcony. "Coward," he yelled. "Hiram warned me he might be attached to you, but I refused to believe it."

Stomping to the desk he opened the top drawer and pulled out a pistol. "As usual I have to do everything myself."

"I've called a press conference. They are setting up on the front lawn now. How do you plan to explain my death?"

Disbelieving her, Linus sputtered. With the gun pointed in her direction he sidled across the room to the window that faced the front yard. "You bitch. You think you can ruin me? You were nothing but a whore when I found you, willing to sell your body for money. And now you're blackmailing me?"

He'd lost, but it wasn't a victory that gave

her joy. Like fruit suspended in gelatin, both waited for an action to free them. Linus fingered the drape and scrutinized the front lawn a second time. She didn't have to peer out the window to know the press were arriving the furrowed brow and grimace on her husband's face told her he didn't like what was happening below.

His secrets were about to be spilled. Although his mind raced to think of an answer, there was nothing he could do.

"Where are the guards?" he mumbled more to himself than to her. He pressed the intercom button on the phone. "Who's in the kitchen?"

No reply. He tried the guard house at the front gate and their sleeping quarters over the garage to the same effect. He was alone. Tears sprang to his eyes, causing Nicole's pity to swell.

"You cunt. You stupid, ignorant whore. You're only a useless woman." He aimed the gun at her again. "No one will care. With you dead I can bluff my way out of this."

"Except for the recording."

His eyes widened. "What are you talking about?"

She pointed toward her purse. "Smile for the camera."

He huffed out a guffaw. "You think I can't destroy that?"

"Despite your attempts to isolate me, I'm not alone. That device is attached to a computer and if you kill me, my death will be breaking news within minutes."

The Senator's face went from true shock to mottled fury. "Bitch." Spittle sprayed from his lips with each word. "I saved you. Without me you would have been ruined."

Nicole said nothing. Arguing the facts would have been a waste of energy. Linus marched to the window again and stared at the ground. She measured the distance to the door. If she could get to the hallway, Austin would help her. She stopped. Linus was already doomed. If she led him to the hallway, he would kill him as well. She raised her chin and stood taller not daring to move. Alive, Austin would see Libby was safe and Linus was arrested.

"It's over, Linus. Give up."

Tears streaked his mottled face. "I deserved better." He turned the gun toward her. While he had flourished it with vicious intent for several minutes, now he held it steady, aimed at her heart. Pure hatred filled his features.

Her eyes closed as her knees buckled, and her body collapsed to the floor. Nicole bit her lips to keep from screaming, fearful that any noise of distress would have Austin bursting through the door. A shot, louder than she could have possibly imagined, filled the room.

She forced her eyes open. Boots were everywhere. Three men appeared at her side, lifting her to her feet. They had been in the room all along. She'd never been alone. Austin wrapped his arms around her and turned her into his chest.

But Nicole had to see. Her husband lay in a crumpled heap on the floor. A lumpy red splatting of blood oozed down the wall.

Zack kicked the gun by the dead man's side across the room. Travis picked up the desk phone and dialed 9-1-1. "I'm calling to report a suicide."

Austin had lifted her into his arms and found a wingback chair. She was now settled on his lap with his strong arms around her.

"You are the bravest woman I know. My heart stopped. I had him in my sights and could have taken him out at any time, but you needed to play it out until the end. It killed me. I love you."

She curled next to him unable to speak, content to let the flow of his words warm her frozen heart.

"I love you," he repeated. "I've loved you since the moment we met."

She stroked his cheek then turned to assess the room.

"I was prepared to take him out if he moved on you, but instead he turned the gun on himself. Before any of us could tackle him, he fired. I thought you didn't know what was wrong with the Super Pac."

She shook her head and mumbled. "I didn't. I still don't, but he acted so weird about it, I decided it couldn't be on the up and up." She sagged against his chest.

"Is she okay?" Travis asked.

"She will be. We need to get her out of here." His hand stroked her back.

The nightmare was over. Linus was dead. Libby was safe. Austin loved her. She repeated the litany over and over in her mind. Libby was safe. Austin loved her.

She'd told her mother she loved him, but she'd never used the words to tell him. "Marry me, Jim Jones. I love you and want to spend my life with you."

A hoot came from across the room, but neither Austin nor Nicole looked to see who'd made the noise.

"Cathy Jones. Nicole Layton. The name doesn't matter. 'A rose by any other name would smell as sweet.' What matters is that I get to spend the rest of my life with you and Libby."

Nicole buried her head in his shoulder.

Travis grunted. "You're quoting

Shakespeare? No wonder I can't convince Abby to marry me."

Zack laughed. "You have no romance in your soul." Then turning to Austin, he added, "And you have too much. She can't marry right away. Widow one day, bride the next, will keep her in the news."

Austin frowned. "As Rhett Butler famously said, 'I can't wait all my life to catch you between husbands'."

Nicole laughed softly. "You can relax. I'm not marrying anyone but you."

She was safe, but more than anything else she was in love. Her Mr. Jones wanted her. There were details to clean up, but she had time. And she'd have Libby. She kissed him lightly on the lips and he responded with a fierce kiss that left her breathless.

"Stop that," Travis said. "We've got press outside, and Nicole needs to make a statement."

She climbed off Austin's lap and readjusted her clothes. "What happened to Gunter?"

"Travis took him out. He's behind the couch."

"Took him out? He's dead?" How many people had to die before she could completely free of Linus? She read the faces of the men. Every one of them believed he deserved to die. There was no remorse in this room. "If you were here all along, why didn't I see you?"

Austin snaked his arm around her waist. "We're SEALs, honey. Well, ex-SEALs. This is what we do. Are you ready to address the media?"

She shook her head. "I haven't thought about what to say."

"Surprise them." Austin's eyes crinkled. "Tell them the truth."

Police arrived on the scene and allowed Nicole a few sentences before ushering the press off the lawn. She gave the police an equally short statement. Austin offered them a tape of everything that happened and promised if they needed her Nicole would be available.

Travis oversaw the proceedings from the edge of the lawn. Zack and Sam joined him as things were wrapping up. "You're driving back to Indianapolis?" He asked Zack.

"I am. It's only a few hours. I don't want Chloe to spend another night alone."

The men embraced. "Thanks for coming. Being together again was like old times. If you're ever interested you have a job waiting."

"Appreciate it. With a kid on the way, I'm staying close to home, but thanks for letting me play in your sandbox." Zack sauntered off with a brief wave.

"So how did you really know to come?"

Travis asked Sam when they were alone.

"Abby was worried about you."

Travis didn't even bother to mask his surprise. "Abby called you?" She hadn't appeared that concerned when she kissed him good-bye.

"Not exactly." Sam scuffed his shoe in the gravel. "I dropped by to see you."

Silence followed. Travis waited, knowing Sam would tell him in his own way.

"I quit the department."

"For good or a leave of absence?" Travis had known he wasn't happy.

"They left the door open for me, but I don't think I can go back."

Sam also had an open invitation to work with the security company, so Travis didn't bother to repeat it.

"I have things in Missouri I need to take care of. I'm headed there next."

Missouri? This had something to do with Skid Rowe's death. It had been five years, but today was the closest Travis had seen of The Cube's younger personality. Visiting Missouri might be the thing Sam needed to overcome his ghosts. "If there's anything we can do, let us know."

"You guys are always my wing men. Are you flying home?"

"Yeah."

"I'll clean out the van and get the equipment to Portland, but it might take awhile."

"Thanks." Since he didn't ask about a ride, Travis assumed Zack had already offered. He watched his friend, a man as close as a true brother, walk away and never had he felt so alone.

Austin thumped his back and drew him into a hug. "Great strategy."

"Partners."

"Forever."

"Sam quit the force and is on his way to Missouri."

"About time. Nicole needs to stay for a few days to put things in order. Libby will eventually be flown to Chicago so we can pick her up there. Shouldn't be more than a week or so." Austin stared across the lawn. "Well, well. Look who's here."

Hiram Lynch side-stepped the police and the tail end of the press as he headed toward the brothers. His was not a look of friendliness. There was no doubt he heard the news about his client.

When he was within earshot but not close enough to shake hands, he stopped and stuffed his hands in his pockets. The fingers on the right hand moved continuously, making Travis think the stories he'd heard about Lynch's superstitions might be true.

"That's twice," Lynch said. "The third time you interfere with my business will not end with a warning." Before either man could respond he walked away.

"That sounded like a threat," Austin said.

"Really, I thought it was the sound of a gauntlet being tossed."

"We needed a challenge. I wonder what else we can do to piss him off."

# THANK YOU!

Thanks for reading The Wrong Husband, the fourth book in the Wrong Series where Wrong Never Felt So Right. I truly hoped you enjoyed it.

If you liked this book, tell a friend, write a review, or send an email. If you hated this book, tell me why. Let me know where I failed to value your time. I welcome any comments you would like to make.

If you would like to be notified of the next book in this series. Please go to my website at: www.Nancybrophy.com and sign up for my newsletter.  Or you can email me at: Nancybrophy@gmail.com. I appreciate hearing from readers.

## About the Author:

Nancy Brophy lives in Portland, Oregon. She, her husband, her two dogs, PB and J, and forty chickens own a house that was destroyed by fire. Fourteen hair-pulling months later they've moved back into the house. One day she'll be able to laugh about it. Then she'll use it in a story.

Stories don't get written by themselves.

The following people played a major role in bringing this story to life: Cassiel Knight, Su Lute, Linda Mercury, Jessie Smith, and Linda Kearney.

A special thanks to my good friends, Austin and Nicole, who took the time to tell me their story.

Nancy would love to hear from you.

www.nancybrophy.com
Nancybrophy@gmail.com